More books by Greg Cornwell

Twilight – A defence of death with dignity

The John Order Series:

Order and the Suspect Suicide

Order and Mrs Cohen's Conviction

Order and the Abandoned Body

Order and the Merimbula Mystery

Order and the Luckless Lovers

Order and the Parliamentary Conference

Order and the Motel Murder

Order and the Curse Crime

JOHN ORDER POLITICIAN & SLEUTH SERIES BOOK 2

GREG CORNWELL

ORDER

AND MRS COHEN'S CONVICTION

Copyright © 2021 Greg Cornwell

ISBN: 978-1-922565-04-4
Published by Vivid Publishing
A division of Fontaine Publishing Group
P.O. Box 948, Fremantle
Western Australia 6959
www.vividpublishing.com.au

Cataloguing-in-Publication data is held at the National Library of Australia.

To all who have stood for preselection

ONE

"It's Mrs. Cohen," said Liz through the intercom.

John Order, member of the Australian Capital Territory parliament thanks to a 176 by-election majority, lifted the receiver and punched the rectangle beside the triangle.

"Mrs. Cohen."

"It's Mrs. Cohen, Mr. Order," the elderly Jewish lady repeated with a slight accent. "Have you seen today's paper?"

It was a glorious early autumn Canberra day with no wind; otherwise the daily newspaper would have blown away upon delivery. The flyaway, Tuesday's edition was called.

"Well, yes," he began, feeling the thin broadsheet between his fingers.

"The boy. The boy who fell from the hotel balcony. Page three. I knew him."

"Oh, I'm so sorry, Mrs. Cohen."

"I must see you."

"Let me check my diary." Order had learned in his brief time as an elected representative it did not pay to be too eager to visit constituents. You had to give the impression you were busy about wider electorate concerns, even if you were not.

"It's urgent, Mr. Order. I think he was pushed."

Manoeuvring carefully from beside Eddie Brown's Commodore, badly parked as usual, Order wondered how Mrs. Cohen could hold such a suspicion.

The details were brief. A young man, thought to be a guest, had fallen to his death the previous night from the balcony of a city hotel. Police were investigating.

Yet Mrs. Cohen was not a person to reach silly conclusions, he decided, changing lanes upon Commonwealth Avenue bridge in a burst of impatience at the slower driver ahead. And unlike many old people, she didn't complain unnecessarily nor expect the impossible.

The cracked pavements and uncut grass he could accept and action as a politician, but refereeing arguments with neighbours or firing someone else's bullet of cantankerousness soon dispelled the myth of benign old people. Many were nasty, selfish and demanding no matter what the socially concerned liked to put around during Seniors' Week.

But Mrs. Cohen was okay, he knew, as he turned into her street of old weatherboard houses dozing in the sun, placidly awaiting death from developers.

A contact established from his regular weekend doorknocking campaign - you can't be complaisant with a 176 majority as Bernie, the Party secretary, continually reminded him – Mrs. Cohen had sought his help upon several occasions. Now the broken pavements had been repaired and were holding up, he noted crossing from the car, while the barking dog had been silenced. The fallen acorns had defeated him as testified by the trees towering along the nature strip.

The lounge room of the guvvie always was a surprise because of its simplicity.

In spite of Bernie's warnings not to go inside when doorknocking, Order was familiar with many standard government housing properties. Often untidy, too many people and too little money, those of the elderly usually were crammed with the possessions of a lifetime, the comfort of the familiar and the attendant memories in old age.

The Cohen lounge room held none of these records of a life. It was neat but sparse.

A couple of paintings, a television, chairs and lounge around a small table, some magazines, his eyes took in a quick sweep but Mrs. Cohen was talking.

"I'm sure it's him, Mr. Order," she said in a quavering voice, the newspaper in her hands.

"How about we sit down an' you start at the beginning, Mrs. Cohen," Order said gently, guiding the old lady to a deep russet-coloured lounge chair directly in front of the TV.

"The beginning, Mr. Order? That would be a long long way back." Order thought the eyes took on a vacant look, but the woman continued: "To pre-war Poland."

"I'm seventy five, Mr. Order, but even so I can't tell you much about that time."

Mrs. Cohen had offered him nothing to eat or drink. She just sat huddled and leaning slightly forward in her seat.

"I was born in Warsaw. I was too young to know what happened in the war, except that it was a miracle I survived when most others did not. That's why the Levy boy's visit came as a shock. I thought they all died."

"We were neighbours, you see. A big apartment building. Stone. I remember the lift." She smiled depreciatingly. "I still find these single storey houses with land in Australia so strange, even after all these years."

Order said nothing, remembering the youthful overseas visit to Europe, post-school, pre-university, and the shock of apartment-style living which characterised the cities.

"We were neighbours," she continued, "and we socialised because the children were about the same age. Old Mr. Levy, the grandfather in my time, was in business, in precious stones. Diamonds of course. We Jews are great diamond merchants."

"Then it happened," Mrs. Cohen said simply. "I was so lucky. I was taken to the country. Perhaps my father sensed something and the countryside was safer. I survived the war and everything else thanks to Polish people who were not even Jewish."

"Afterwards we fled, the Russians I mean - Poles hate the Russians - and in a displaced persons' camp in Austria at seventeen I met my husband, another survivor 'though he *was* in a concentration camp. We married and came here to Australia because it was so far away."

"The Levy boy, Mrs. Cohen?" Order prompted.

"Yes, of course. The past is for us older people."

"The Levy's disappeared for me when I was sent to the country and they remained but an occasional pleasing addition to a limited childhood memory of a tall - everything is tall or big when you're young, Mr. Order - stone building with a lift. "

"The Levy's are part of the memory because there is so little to remember. I really thought that like my family they'd all died, but you hold on to what little you have of the past. Like an old girlfriend, eh?"

"The Levy boy, Mrs. Cohen?" a blushing Order encouraged.

"Yes. Well as you know as a politician, we Jewish residents of Canberra keep in touch with each other. There's not many of us but the group is kind to older people like me."

"I don't know how he found me. Someone here with contacts in Israel - some of our people have migrated back there, you know - possibly recalled the ramblings of an old woman about her youth. I haven't had time to check, he saw me only yesterday and now he's dead."

"The body hasn't been identified."

"I understand that. The newspaper was vague as usual, but I know it's Daniel Levy."

"Howso?"

"He came here to see somebody, Mr. Order. Came from Israel to where his surviving family must have moved from Europe."

"But why an' who did he want to see?"

"I don't know the why - although he talked about justice - and he only had a Polish name which meant nothing to me."

"People often anglicise their name when they migrate."

"That's what I thought and why I asked you to come and see me."

"To check out the name?"

"Of course. And the reason. Daniel Levy is dead, Mr. Order. You see he had an appointment last night at his hotel and I suspect it was with the person of the Polish name."

"Which is?"

"Korzeniowski, I understand. Here, Daniel wrote it down for me."

As Mrs. Cohen leaned forward to give Order the paper she checked her movement.

"You alright, Mrs. Cohen?" Order half rose from the depths of his lounge chair.

"Tablet, Mr. Order." Her voice was strained, she obviously had difficulty breathing and resorted to pointing with an unsteady finger to a small container on the table.

"Water?"

Mrs. Cohen nodded.

In the kitchen out back he found a teacup, brought it through half full, opened the plastic container and gave both cup and a tablet to the pale old lady.

"Thank you," she said after drinking. "My heart."

"No, no. I don't need a doctor. My turns look worse than they really are. Thank you again for your help."

"I'd better be going, Mrs. Cohen, so you can rest. I'll see what I can find out about your Polish name. You realise it might not have anything to do with Daniel Levy's death - if it was him who fell."

"It was him alright, I sense it. Just as I'm sure he was pushed. You will help me, Mr. Order?"

"Of course. But why did he contact you, Mrs. Cohen? He had the name, or a name, already. Surely any reasonably well-informed member of your Jewish community here could have helped him?"

Mrs. Cohen's smile was sad, Order recollected, as he looked up at the turning and falling leaves of the oaks and thought of tall stone buildings across the world more than half a century ago.

"Perhaps he wanted to meet someone who knew his lost family," she had said.

TWO

"So he did get the address from you, Mr. Reynolds?" Funny name for a Jew but that was whom his friend Ben had suggested he call. "No, there's no problem at all. It's just that Mrs. Cohen is a constituent an' she was curious. Lydia Cohen? Well, I suppose that's her but I've never known her first name. No, I agree. A very proper old lady with whom you'd never be that familiar."

An idea came to Order. "Look, to be sure, did you meet this Daniel Levy? Did he come to the Jewish Centre an' if so, can you describe him? I can tell Mrs. Cohen an' hopefully she'll confirm if it was the same man."

Bulky body, short thick legs - he'd appeared at the Centre *in shorts* - dark hair and glasses. Volatile, much given to waving his hands when excited. And he was very excited, Mr. Order, he recalled Reynolds saying. He'd tracked down the man he was looking for and was arranging a meeting. No, it must have been Sunday he'd seen Levy, couldn't have been Saturday because that is our Sabbath, you understand.

"Did you know Mrs. Cohen's first name is Lydia, Liz?" Order called through to his secretary's office.

And Liz, middle-aged, divorced and super efficient, who was not given to gossip or trivial conversation, said she hadn't, and then added: "Bernie's phoned and it's on."

"When?"

"Advertisement's this Saturday for next Monday and closing Monday fortnight."

"Two weeks? That's not much time."

"You've been expecting it for at least a month. Everyone has and if you're all not ready now, you never will be."

Nothing had been said at yesterday's parliamentary Party meeting but that was to be expected. The executive, who made the decision in conjunction with members of the Party administration, now met after the elected members had held their meeting. This was not always the case, however recently a rare backbench rebellion had been successful in demanding the Party room be consulted before the executive decided upon policy matters, thus seriously weakening the inner sanctum's power.

The defeat had not been forgotten and regrettably, the change did not extend to administrative matters.

"D'you reckon calling candidates now for preselection means an early election?"

"Who knows? Rumours have been around for months, John," Liz said, using his first name as she did when they were alone. "If I can borrow your car, I'll pick up the form from Bernie. The sooner we get cracking, the faster we make the deadline."

"Go ahead."

Interesting that there was no question he would *not* stand again, thought Order, back at his desk to decide how many of the twenty names could be contacted quickly of Party members living in the electorate he needed to endorse his application for the preselection opportunity.

It was a bloody nuisance having to go through the rigmarole of filling in the document as if you were a tyro when you were the sitting member, but that was democracy.

Anyway, most of the responses to the form's not very original questions already were on file from the last time. They only needed updating: adding a few patron positions and club and society memberships.

And Liz was correct. There was no way he would *not* stand again. Nobody who has been elected in a by-election would refuse the chance to win in their own right in a general election.

No matter how remote the likelihood of winning again: a fortuitous victory achieved because of a candidate in a blue ribbon seat forgetting to nominate, a personal scandal requiring the incumbent suddenly to resign or, in his own case, the death of the sitting government member thus requiring a by-election when the Government was unpopular. Whatever, you as the member had to run again because your Party demanded it of you.

And sometimes you got lucky.

An untimely death in a *marginal* seat at the wrong time occasionally gave the opposition - Government or big O opposition - the chance to win and subsequently the chance to retain the seat.

It was this that drove John Order, as it had driven dozens perhaps hundreds of candidates before him.

The second time around if you had won the seat by good fortune previously, you owed it to yourself, never mind the Party, to stand again and to win again, simply to prove you could do so without some divine intervention.

"I didn't use all that shoe leather doorknocking to pull out now," Order justified quietly to himself as he searched in a cabinet in Liz's office for his file and its original preselection statement.

But first the twenty all important signatures. Those closest would be the easiest obviously, which meant here in parliament house.

His friend Rob Glasson's secretary was one, King's woman, whatever her name was another. And Avril, Fearless Leader's front desk girl. Jim Terry, public relations and media officer for the Opposition backbenchers and probably a few more too. Liz would know.

In the unlikely event he was challenged for preselection, those who signed his application were neither obliged nor committed to vote for him. This sensible understanding saved embarrassment and probably lasting enmity, because a simple requirement fraught with such political factionalism and personal prejudices otherwise would make family or neighbourhood feuds friendship societies by comparison.

It only calls for current Party membership and residence in the electorate, he again reminded himself.

While waiting for Liz to return, Order decided Mrs. Cohen's request could be advanced. As the next stop was the police he dialled his contact, the laconic Detective Inspector Williams.

"Gabby? John Order."

"G'day, John."

"Gabby, I need your help," Order ploughed on, ignoring the cautious greeting and the following silence, which gave the man his ironic nickname.

"Can you make some enquiries for me?" Order asked, after he had explained Mrs. Cohen's concerns. "D'you know who's in charge of the matter?"

"Intimately. I am."

"Great. Then you *can* help me. Mrs. Cohen -"

"It's a clear case," Williams stressed the words with slow deliberation, "of accidental death."

"He had an appointment last night."

"So? Probably had a few drinks. Went out for some fresh air. Happens a lot with young men."

"I don't think Jewish people drink very much, Gabby."

"Wait for the autopsy. He's been deceased for less than twenty four hours."

"I really would appreciate it, Gabby, if you could help me set an old woman's concerns to rest. As I told you, it goes back to the Second World War. Poland. He'd been here a few days an' it wasn't a social visit, as I explained. I don't want to be a nuisance."

"No, you never intend to be," Gabby said glumly. "I'll see what I can do."

Liz appeared at the door, stopping when she saw he was speaking upon the telephone. Order waved her forward.

"Thanks, Gabby. I really do appreciate it." There could have been a grunt before the line was disconnected.

"Trying to put Mrs. Cohen's mind to rest," Order explained.

"Let's hope you have better luck with her than with yourself," Liz said grimly. "Here's your application and would you sign this one."

"This is my electorate," Order said, accepting the papers. "Why two?"

The implication hit him even as Liz spelled it out.

"You're being challenged for preselection, John. Your old foes, the Bennett's."

"That bastard's never forgiven me for beating him in the by-election preselection an' he's been trying to white-ant me ever since. Okay Bob, I've done for you once an' I'll do for you again."

"It's not Bob, John. It's his wife, Lorraine."

THREE

"That fat bitch."

"Plump, John," corrected Bernie, perhaps displaying an unadmitted attraction, "an' don't go saying that again *anywhere*."

Bernie, the balding, chain-smoking Party secretary, old, shy in public but very effective upon a telephone, continued: "You've a fight on your hands, John. While you were preoccupied with various types of bodies - the Melville's for example - Lorraine and Bob have been quietly working the branches, particularly the women."

"But I'm the sitting member an' holding on by my fingernails. How could the Executive allow this, risking such a marginal seat?"

"You did support the party room revolt, I hear," said Bernie who heard everything. "Perhaps you offended some of our powerful political figures and they want to make an example?"

"Why me?" Now he was aggrieved.

"Why not? Last in, first out, perhaps? Expediency? A pledge of loyalty if elected which you didn't demonstrate?"

"Ungrateful bastards!"

"Enough John. Don't just remember what I told you month's ago but also accept that in politics you have many acquaintances but few friends."

"I'll fight."

"Of course you will. You've no choice. Hit the phones an' start shoring up your support. I've given Liz - as I do any candidate - the list of eligible paid-up members who can vote in the preselection. So go for it."

"That - Lorraine's got a hide asking me to sign her application."

"Psychological warfare an' there's only one way to neutralize it."

"Howso?"

"Get her an' Bob to sign yours. There's no commitment an' I don't think they'd dare say no. You'd make capital out of their refusal."

"Good one, Bernie. I'll get onto it immediately."

"One more thing, John. Stay clear of Mike Prentice."

"Mike? He's my runner. Old friend. Essential."

"Not any more. He's working for Lorraine. I told you you had a fight on your hands."

"Liz!" he called impatiently, replacing the receiver.

"Mike Prentice has gone over to the Bennett's. We've a fight on our hands. How much time have we got before the actual preselection?"

"No date set, according to Bernie."

To give all candidates time to lobby, thought Order, without cluttering the field with the hopeful and the hopeless. If you couldn't get your twenty signatures in a fortnight, you were out.

He'd always regarded Lorraine as the stronger of the Bennett's. Seeing them together you wondered why a woman like her, tough and capable, had married someone like Bob. By comparison he was a mouse. Was it love, simply procreation or dominance?

Whatever, he now realised he was much more confident of winning the preselection last time facing Bob and not Lorraine.

"We hit the phones, Liz. Find out how many preselectors on the list with business or only home numbers."

"I'll phone ahead?"

"No. This has to be a person-to-person call. An' see if I can decently cancel any electoral appearances, in case I've to visit some of the preselection voters. Don't actually cancel anything; just let's see what's on that I might have to give a miss."

Attendance at electoral events: community, multicultural, social, all took a back seat to a fight for political survival. After all, if you weren't there, you were no use to any public organization.

"You want everyone who can vote?"

"Yeah. Even the Bennett's supporters. But star them, Liz, so I know I'm in enemy territory an' I'll phone them last. No point tipping off my opponent until she has to find out."

"When's Jayson in?" he added.

It was a standing joke. Jason with a pretentious y. The gofer from the university who worked part-time.

"Tomorrow."

"Get him to bring forward the electorate letter we've been planning. I'll need it out within the next say, two weeks?"

"Before the preselection?"

"Hopefully. The party punters - or most of them - along with everyone else need to receive it before preselection to give them evidence I'm doing something."

Before Liz could reply, Order again added: "An' tell Jayson I'm under preselection challenge. Be subtle but make it clear his part-time job's on the line if I loose. His university Party mates in my seat will be useful to my survival."

Lunch in the parliamentary dining room was at best a somber location. For whatever reason - the no smoking rule, the increased committee workload usually in the afternoons when the House wasn't sitting, the conscientious women members, social changes between generations - there were no long lunches anymore.

"I'm okay," said Rob Glasson, two term member and Order's friend, sipping a lonely glass of red wine in the almost empty room.

"Glad to hear," said Order, playing with his rapidly cooling lasagna.

"You've a fight on your hands."

"Yeah." If he heard that comment again he'd …

Mike Prentice. Tall and lean, like Order. Happily married but popular with the women and a good bloke with the men. Order's runner in the previous preselection, tireless worker during the by-election campaign, drinking buddy, confidant in the late night strategy sessions and Order's driver on the big day itself, when he toured the polling booths to give a morale boost to his workers.

"Rob, the Bennett's have always had it in for me, I know, but Prentice? He was my right-hand man during the campaign. Helped me get the votes for the preselection win. I've known Mike for years. He was my mate!"

The ultimate accolade.

Rob Glasson looked across the vacant spaces of the dining room, the absence of other members giving a privacy usually lacking during sittings.

"Maybe he wants to be on a winner, John," Glasson said gently. "Not everyone has principles in this game."

Even you have doubts then about my chances of success, thought Order.

"Perhaps I could ring Carol an' find out why he's switched?" Order believed he'd always had a strong - although not *as* strong - friendship with Prentice's wife.

"No can do. She's in Sydney with their daughter, who's just had her first baby. Carol - my Carol - told me."

There was a network among the spouses of members, exclusively wives, to which Order as a bachelor had no access. It was informal and not all embracing, quirky sometimes, with the partners of factional opponents' firm friends while those of factional supporters cool toward each other. Some, like the right wing maverick George Graham's wife, were card-carrying members of the 'other party', or spouses of such as the Whip, Harold Chambers, or of sleepy Finlay, nobody ever saw.

So with his wife away Judas Prentice can work his charm upon my women voters, unbecoming as many of them are, thought Order.

"Incidentally, she got you this," Glasson slid a glossy pamphlet across to him. "Lorraine was handing them out at a Women's Institute lunch an' Carol thought you might like a copy."

Lorraine Bennett's flyer showed a not unattractive woman, even if the photo was of a younger person without the emerging double chin, Order noted unchivalrously. Full lips, generous smile, even the nose was appealing. The hair, of course, was immaculate. The copy was very low-key. No claims which could not be substantiated, no promises impossible to fulfil and no personal details which could be questioned.

Bland and threatening, Order recognised.

"Time to go. Planning committee meeting. Take care, John," Glasson placed his glass upon the table, "an' good luck. You've got a fight on your hands."

FOUR

"The Kerrigan's are overseas, John White's in hospital an' Mrs. Wilberforce isn't financial because she's resigned again over something or other," Order complained, frowning at his well-scribbled membership list.

"She'll be back. Always is."

"Not soon enough to vote for me, Liz."

"I've got the twenty signatures, including Lorraine Bennett, so that's a chore out of the way."

"How did she react?"

"Nothing. Not a word." Liz paused. "Ran into her in the corridor earlier."

"An' with whom?"

"Julie Davenport."

Order pursed his lips, fighting the temper building inside him. Bloody Davenport. A Party wet and his fellow opposition member on the Education Committee.

Seeing his expression, Liz continued: "Hardly surprising, is it? The sisterhood will stick together. They're always pushing for more women in parliament."

Affirmative action to elect more women had gone underground in most political parties in recent years but it remained a powerful force. Few female members were not influenced to some extent by its beguiling attraction, particularly when they became the target of male insensitivity or plain arrogance.

"Paul Severin's playing games too. He won't commit himself to support me. Then, casual like, raises the difficulty of getting enough votes in the party room for a motion against graffitists. Why can't the bloody old Tory live in his own damned electorate?"

"Where's Jayson?" he asked to change the subject in the following silence. "It's Wednesday."

"He's out chasing some photos for your electoral newsletter. I've spoken to him about uni support."

"And?"

"Non-committal. But don't read too much into it. He doesn't think there are many votes there anyway. Most of the students like to shack up on campus or at least away from home. He said he'd do his best."

"Williams' got back yet?" Remembering his own promise to Mrs. Cohen.

"I'll let you know." And motherly, added: "Why don't you take a break, John? Get out of the office for a while? A walk around the block? Now we've got the twenty signatures we can pace ourselves calling in the votes. We don't even have a preselection date yet."

"I can't afford to be complaisant, Liz. Not with the Bennett's marshalling their forces."

"But you can't appear over-anxious either. You're the sitting member, the by-election hero. If you start heavying people too soon they'll begin to wonder if you're up to it, that your victory was a fluke and you a oncer. You've got the track record, don't throw the advantage away."

Order recognised the commonsense of her argument. With no preselection date announced there was a long way to go. And people were fickle. Anything could happen between now and D Day to change their voting intention. Nobody could be guaranteed so far out.

He also knew some rank and file party members took perverse

pleasure in making preselection candidates sweat for their support. The old Australian game of cutting down a tall poppy.

As the sitting member, Order was the tallest poppy, but he also understood why people who worked uncomplainingly at polling booths, who attended the often deadly boring branch meetings, who stayed loyal despite the inevitable public falls in Party popularity, enjoyed their once in every few years chance to make their sitting member or an aspirant take notice of their essential role.

"Okay. Let me proofread what we've got for the newsletter an' I'll take the rest of the day off," he conceded.

It was not to be.

Like the papers piling up in his in-tray.

In spite of Liz's ruthless culling of magazines, journals and periodicals from all over the country as well as the local contributions, Order still acquired a sizeable amount of printed material needing his personal examination. Most went in the wastepaper bin beside his desk, about ten percent he read briefly and of this about two percent called for his full attention.

And then there were the e-mails.

"You can't take the afternoon off, John," Liz explained through the intercom. "You've education at three."

Which I'd forgotten, thought Order irritably. And I've to sit with that bitch Davenport.

The company of Julie Davenport did not appeal at the best of times, but she was particularly trying in committee meetings.

He was constantly attempting to check her enthusiastic efforts to bring out the best in people, who usually - at least in his opinion - professed to have the government's interests, thus read their own, at heart. An unashamed wet she was a nuisance.

With Davenport around, one needed a purgative.

Rabbit.

He recalled with irony he'd met her at an education seminar, which Davenport as the senior opposition committee member should have attended but was unable to do so. First day at school for her youngest child, he remembered with gratitude.

Rabbit too was present by accident, filling in for a sick superior. They had hit it off from the first coffee break of an otherwise forgettable day. A day of inspirational papers delivered badly by people who had not written them and presented to an audience which was not really committed because they realised they could never financially act upon the suggestions.

It was easy money for the seminar organisers and a sexual triumph for Rabbit and John Order. Within days they were lying companionably in bed, lust temporarily satiated.

Rabbit - her real name was June or Janet or something like that - was married to a husband who worked in Sydney during the week, returning home at weekends. Their two children were at boarding school in the southern highlands of New South Wales.

It was, as he admitted, made to order.

They met at her home, his flat, occasionally neutral locations like a small out-of-town motel. He enjoyed the clandestine meetings, the risk, and the danger of being seen.

It was sheer lust, often not pausing to remove all of their clothes. No commitment, no love - Order couldn't even remember afterwards what her body looked like when they did get completely naked. Just wild, free sex.

But no longer uncomplicated, because if the Bennett's found out about the association he was done.

A bachelor parliamentarian was acceptable so long as his private life was that of a celibate. Certainly he could be seen in public with a woman, but not too often or tongues would wag about probable nuptials and, if no wedding, a mistress perhaps or was he gay?

While this was the general view, enlightened Canberra society did not really question the intimate details of such arrangements *unless* they were brought to attention.

Crudely put, if the Bennett's found out he was screwing Rabbit, a married woman, and quietly spread the information, Order himself would be screwed for a preselection win from the party members.

And now there was a problem too with Rabbit, Order realised, surrounded to his left by mounting paperwork he no longer had time to address, a scribbled over list of party members before him and an empty out-tray to his right. Everything was sacrificed if political survival was at stake.

Rabbit was not political. In fact, apart from asking him why he was at the seminar and what he did, she had never asked anything about him again. No time, Order thought, with a grin.

The problem was if he continued the lustful association and the Bennett's did find out it could ruin his political career. On the other hand, if he closed it down now and Rabbit got angry, she could do the same, with or without the Bennett's help.

Still, the preselection date had not been announced, it was Wednesday and he would have a difficult time sitting next to Julie Davenport during the committee meeting.

Maybe he and Rabbit *could* have a last fling upon this, one of their regular nights and give him a chance to explain the situation.

Order picked up the telephone.

FIVE

"I wonder what took them so long," Liz mused.

It was shaping up to be another beautiful early autumn day. Canberrans justifiably claimed the seasons between summer's heat and winter's cold made living in the National Capital worthwhile. From his window Order could see the leaves of the claret ash beginning to colour, although not to the same shade as his face.

"Jim Terry had better handle this. I'm not sure I could manage a personal appearance without saying something wrong."

"Not as if it's a major news story. I'm not the first to be challenged for preselection," he grumbled.

"Nor the only member this time around. Our Education Minister, Bob Craddock, is rumoured to be challenged by the sisterhood, I hear."

"Good point, Liz. He could take some of the heat off me. But they haven't called nominations yet."

Politicians are like some wild beasts. If they see one who is weak, even one of their own, they'll pull them down. And Craddock was particularly suitable being in government.

"A quiet night's done you the world of good, John. You're thinking very positively. We should ask Jim to put out a broadcast statement to save the other media outlets phoning up."

"Something simple but confident," Order agreed unconvincingly. "Anybody's democratic right to nominate. That sort of thing. Terry will know what to say."

"I'll see to it."

Order settled down to proofread the electorate newsletter copy and check through the photographs Jayson had collected yesterday. There were four pictures: two of him at functions and two with constituents who Order hoped would not be recognised by too many voters as party members and personal friends.

"Try not to have your photo taken looking happy or doing some fun thing," Bernie had counselled during the previous successful campaign, "an' never being gleeful or wearing a silly hat. The media will use it for everything from a child's tragic death to the announcement of World War Three."

"How about sending them one of my own?" he had asked in political ignorance.

"That they'll only use for your obituary. They know it's staged."

He was deliberating whether or not to use a photograph with Mike Prentice squatting beside him at a gross pollutant trap site when Liz put through DI Williams.

"Gabby."

"He checked in on Friday," Williams said without preliminaries. "We're trying to contact next-of-kin. In Israel. We found a passport."

"So Mrs. Cohen was right. It is Levy."

"I didn't mention a name, John."

"Any idea who he saw Monday night?"

"The desk says nobody asked for his room number."

So it must have been a pre-arranged appointment, thought Order.

"Any phone calls?"

"A couple. Jewish Centre."

"And?"

"And I've said enough."

"Come on Gabby!"

"I've told you more than I should already an' we've still to advise the next-of-kin."

"Must have been wealthy. That hotel doesn't come cheap."

"I wouldn't know, John. Out of my league. Perhaps they've tourist weekend rates."

"Credit cards? Papers? Names an' addresses?"

"Enough," said the policeman and hung up.

Either Gabby was not saying or the mysterious Korzeniowski name or any accompanying written details had disappeared from the dead young man's hotel room.

Liz looked in. "Coming through on an e-mail any minute."

"What? " Order was thinking of Mrs. Cohen.

"Jim Terry wants you to okay the statement about your preselection challenge," she said patiently.

"Is that secure? An e-mail, I mean."

"Does it matter? All Canberra will know about it soon."

And so it proved.

"Always have your newsletters printed in the electorate, John, an' pay on time," was again more sensible advice from Bernie. "Most small businesses have cash flow problems an' sometimes a shortage of work, so it won't do you any harm."

Order personally delivered the copy to the printer and was heartened by the man's unconcerned confidence.

"Some sheila challenging you, Mr. Order? Heard it on the radio. You'll be right though. Next Wednesday okay for this?"

Back at the office a pattern of telephone message slips sat upon his desk.

"I didn't phone you," explained Liz, "but I thought you might like to see the support you've got."

"And the rest," said Order.

A media mention always provoked a response, as if people's memories were prodded into remembering either an outstanding and unresolved request or a matter they had been meaning to take up with him.

Most of the calls were from supporters. Preselection votes he already had. Nevertheless, it was comforting they'd troubled to contact him.

"And Mrs. Boone's still waiting for a bigger guvvie," Liz added, as she tidied into a neat pile the encouraging messages.

"She's on the housing waiting list. I can't do any more."

"Mrs. Cohen also rang," Liz said neutrally, ignoring his trace of temper.

"Tell her I'm out, Liz. I need to think about what I can tell her. I'll ring tomorrow. We still okay for Saturday?"

Once a month Order set up a table and signs at a shopping centre, inviting the public to talk to the local member.

"Yes. You've got Alec Higgins and Julie Davenport. It's Threeways."

All I needed, he thought.

Alec probably was the most foul-mouthed man Order had met in his life. He seemed in a perpetual rage and his words reflected this anger. His sentences were punctuated with crude and often grammatically inappropriate adjectives or nouns which would have done proud an inarticulate lout.

Order was amazed he managed to speak so eloquently and without these unnecessary embellishments in the House and he had noticed the same restraint existed when women were present. He was grateful, for once, Julie Davenport would be with them at the large shopping mall which served each of their electorates.

"How are the volunteers?" These were the supporters who turned out to keep the members' company on what often could be a lonely duty. "Youth group this time, isn't it?"

"Not a great response, John. But it's only Thursday," Liz said soothingly. "You know how it is. Depends how long they party at their watering holes Friday night."

And who they're going to support in this showdown with Lorraine Bennett, thought Order bitterly, as Liz went back to her room to telephone Mrs. Cohen.

The youth branch was a constant source of concern to the Party. An indispensable headache, Bernie called them.

Necessary because it provided the nucleus for future parliamentarians and even if the dropout rate to marriage, career and disaffection was akin to the common cold sweeping through an air-conditioned office, the youth branch recognised its power.

Striven with shifting internecine feuds the branch played passionate politics, advancing radical motions at its always stormy meetings to the despair of the parliamentary wing and to the delight of the media. At contested preselections its qualifying members enjoyed the role of kingmakers; their own perceived but often limited influence eclipsed by ruthlessness which had no regard for political pragmatism and which could undermine friend and foe alike.

Order treated the branch with the same caution as did all of his colleagues.

"I've made an eleven o'clock appointment," Liz called through. "She wants to see you again."

And I've not much to tell her, thought Order, replacing a telephone directory which had no Korzeniowski among its listings.

Unless … But it was too late. The office was closed.

He spent a dispiriting hour ploughing through the accumulated papers upon his desk, dumping most into the wastepaper basket and scrawling short instructions - usually redirections - upon the e-mail snowstorm. This he faced each day but which, with the current preoccupation, now had reached blizzard proportions.

Too many computers owned by too many people with too much time on their hands.

Writing a letter requires effort and you can't be anonymous, an address is needed if you want a reply. Further, the work involved demands you have something worthwhile to say or to complain about.

Now you can send off a short or all too frequently a very long e-mail about anything and everything from potholes to pedophiles with nothing more personal than your name and an unintelligible address punctuated by dots.

Heaven knows what the charities collecting used stamps did these days for supplies. His own quarterly contribution was so small as to be embarrassing.

"News, John," Liz called.

The item came through in the third segment after the usual government announcements and opposition responses, crime reports and vehicle accidents. In silence but with mounting fury he watched with Liz.

"Why?"

"Just a different approach, John. Don't take it to heart. Most people are feeding the kids or cooking their own dinner. And it *was* good file footage of you being sworn in."

"But the bloody three second grab was Lorraine Bennett - live!"

She looked good too. Well presented, confident, with just the right amount of humility that suggested she was taking nothing for granted but would make a very suitable candidate.

"You've a fight on your hands, John," Liz said unnecessarily.

SIX

Threeways was busy on a Saturday morning with the dual income couples who did not have children's sport to juggle, with the young who did not have a part time weekend job in one of the mega supermarkets and with the old and often lonely for human contact crowding through its several entrances.

Years past, political parties would set up shop as near as possible to these entrances as allowed by the multinational that owned the complex, and proceed to harass with a proffered pamphlet every person entering.

Then the realisation dawned that busy people, preoccupied with lists of food and other purchases, were not remotely interested in the zealots' attempts to convert to or to sustain a political position. This observation may have been encouraged by the number of their respective pamphlets found in the rubbish bins inside the centre.

So in a momentous but certainly not agreed to shift, major political parties established themselves with tables, chairs, brochures and signs adjacent to the legal limits allowed at the entrances and waited for interested constituents to approach *them*. Minor parties occasionally appeared and with irritating enthusiasm bailed up the shopping hordes with their pamphlets and with the equally unsuccessful results of the larger parties in the past.

Sometimes it was necessary to curb a volunteer's wish to match this fervour and Order frequently had explained to a new worker - and thus before they became a public nuisance both to him and to the Party - that the rules of engagement were a matter for the public to initiate.

As the name implied Threeways had three entrances, roughly the equivalent of the old Y Plan for the design of the National Capital itself and now, equally roughly, these entrances were enticing openings to a world of shop-until-you-drop for the cashed-up voters of each of the Opposition member's electorates.

Thus Julie Davenport, Alec Higgins and John Order were positioned at their respective accesses of the political compass.

With Order were two party volunteers, the youth branch largely and perhaps suspiciously absent.

Old Bob, was a veteran who could remember the end of the Menzies era, Whitlam and all that followed. Bob politically was like the Thin Red Line at Balaklava, unshakeable in his commitment.

Young Robert, on the other hand, was keen but incautious. He tried to engage Order in loud talk about the failings of the Government, a ploy Order recognised as a means of circumventing the Party's understanding not to politically engage the shoppers with unsolicited propaganda.

When this one-sided conversation got too much, Order sent young Robert off to buy a coffee for each of them and luxuriated in the peace of old Bob's quiet reminiscences of earlier campaigns.

A government stall was nearby, staffed by Party stalwarts Nola and Charlie Breen, who were doing no better in custom than his own public political reference point.

Occasionally people stopped, usually to say hello and overwhelmingly *after* they had shopped. Others waved or nodded greetings as they trundled their laden trolleys past to the car park.

Order wondered if the presence of a government stall indicated an early election. There always were rumours of course, but his own albeit amateur intelligence told him government supporters had not been seen in public like this for months.

Was the Chief Minister, Paddles Porter, planning a snap early election? Was this why the party had called preselection so soon?

Young Robert returned with the coffees and perhaps the caffeine settled down his provocation because Order found he was able to relax and simply be an available parliamentary member, as said the sign beside the collapsible table.

Watching the world go by was one of the informative experiences for a politician publicly flag flying.

Women with children, pushing or herding them along. Bodies now distorted from childbirth, the firm breasts sagging, hips wider and the eyes, windows to the soul, focused exclusively upon their offspring, not the world of anything except their next generation, and no husbands with them.

And the number of Asians. Small people estimated out of proportion to their real numbers in the National Capital because they were so easily recognised. Quiet, unassuming, quick to smile if a circumstance arose because they wanted *no* trouble, thus still betraying their uneasiness in this country, Australia, and this city, Canberra. They always had young children.

Also, he noted because it was a hotter than normal autumn day, the young girls, the teenagers and early twenties, wore thongs upon their feet, giving them a very abrupt stunted look and destroying any shapely ankle or leg.

Then the old men.

Either inappropriately dressed for shopping in coat and tie, retired businessmen, some of whom he knew, who felt naked without the enveloping shield of the corporate world and insisted on keeping up the appearances of a lifestyle long discarded. Or the alternative of old out-of-fashion shirts, of shorts and socks: ankle socks. Nasty ugly show-offs of thin white legs, the socks themselves encased in sandals, scuffed slip-ons or dirty Reeboks.

"Make notes," Bernie had advised him. "So many politicians never follow things up. No shame in having a poor memory and taking a note indicates your genuine interest in the matter."

From time to time this paid off, as happened that quiet morning when an elderly man separated himself from his wife and shopping trolley to enthusiastically shake Order's hand.

"I've been trying for years to get them to put up that Stop sign," he babbled. "Thank you. Thank you for your help."

Order had no idea what the fellow was talking about so he simply smiled graciously. Accepting as his due as an active politician the praise for something he possibly hadn't done was a small reward. The thinnest file in his office was labelled Thanks.

Perhaps it was the accent for Order recalled his second visit yesterday to Mrs. Cohen and the unfinished business he had with her. Old Bob and young Robert had moved away during the exchange with the effusive stranger, so he could think.

The body still had not been officially identified when he saw her. We're still trying to locate next-of-kin, Gabby Williams explained patiently again when he had telephoned before the visit. Not that there was any doubt, as Mrs. Cohen had adamantly stated; now an Israeli passport had been located.

"You must find this Korzeniowski, Mr. Order. He's the killer."

He had confirmed to the agitated old lady as gently as he could, fearing another heart spasm, that that was exactly what he had been trying to do.

However the department had not been helpful. The Privacy Act prevented them from divulging the anglicised name of any migrant, he had been told, with just a gleeful hint of you-should-know-this-already and the rules apply to everyone: we don't make exceptions for bloody politicians.

Which left Stan at the Polish Club as his best and last hope and as he had told the woman, he was meeting him tonight.

"I'll contact you again, Mrs. Cohen," was his parting promise at the doorway looking out and up at the oak trees, "if I've further information. "

If. Order was not confident.

While many immigrants clung tenaciously to their roots, conducting language and cultural classes so that their Australian-born children and grandchildren could learn of and appreciate their heritage, many virtually turned their backs upon the old country and its customs. Occasional lip service was paid during religious celebrations, weddings or funerals out of deference to family sensitivities but otherwise these people wanted to be and were dinkim Aussies.

Without a name listing in the telephone directory, Order decided Korzenoiwski was among the latter.

"Morning, John. Been busy?"

Outside Threeways Julie Davenport's question interrupted his thoughts.

"It's so quiet we thought we'd come around and see how you were doing."

Behind his colleague he saw with rising anger Lorraine Bennett with a handful of her glossy brochures.

Conscious old Bob and young Robert were listening and watching closely, Order civilly returned the greeting, adding to Lorraine it was good of her to give up a Saturday morning to help out at a Party stall.

"Getting to know the punters, John. It's good experience," she replied without a blush.

SEVEN

O rder signed himself in and walked through to the lounge bar area.

The Poles were one of the first ethnic groups to establish a club in Canberra to serve the thirsts and interests of their wave of refugees from communist dominated Eastern Europe post World War II.

At first all of these people, casually lumped together as Balts with no recognition of individual nationalities, these flotsam and jetsam from half a dozen war devastated countries were relocated further south of Canberra to work out of Cooma upon the ambitious Snowy Mountains Hydro-Electric Scheme. And here they laboured until it was built, enduring the harsh seasonal conditions of the searing heat and the bitter cold of the high Monaro.

While many, the job finished, fled back to the civilised climate of Sydney or Melbourne, substantial numbers moved in the late fifties and early sixties an hour up the road to where Canberra, so long a sleepy backwater, finally was being established as the high-profile National Capital of Australia.

There was plenty of work and not the backbreaking tunnelling and dam building of the Snowy. Now it was housing construction to accommodate the Commonwealth public servants and their families being transferred from all over Australia.

And, with a fast growing population, other opportunities presented themselves.

Service industries developed and many of yesterday's Snowy labourers dusted off and resumed pre-war careers, trades and professions. Others set up in new business enterprises, fuelled by the twin expectations of good economic times and a city of transplanted well paid young families.

But it was more than the booming job market which encouraged Europe's refugees to stay. They'd come to like the region from their time on the Snowy. It's proximity to the snowfields and the coast, to the mountains and the plains. Granted, Canberra didn't have the bustle of Sydney nor its sophistication, but the Big Smoke wasn't all that far away, even upon admittedly poor roads.

Canberra was pretty, new and, perhaps most important of all, safe.

Over the years as the city grew and prospered, so too did its ethnic populations and with them the various national associations.

Many of the European countries now represented in the city set up their own clubs where their people could meet and in some cases until a church was built, worship. The Federal Government, which then controlled Canberra, gave land for such ventures at a peppercorn rental.

The thirty years from the sixties was the boom time for the ethnic groups and their cultural monuments, and then their influence upon Canberra's social life began to ebb.

There were several reasons for the decline: the relaxation of gaming laws saw an increase in the number of poker machines a club could operate and the more professional of these bodies took full advantage with some amalgamating to fight rising costs. Poor management saw the closure of others.

However the principle reason for the end of the ethnic influence was falling patronage.

The sons and daughters and the grandsons and granddaughters of the original refugees simply did not share the old country bond of their parents and grandparents. They married outside their nationality; they moved away to new suburbs, they no longer spoke the language of their ethnic background at home. They integrated.

It was ironic the ethnic club demise shortly preceded the politician's discovery of multiculturalism and its perceived capacity to attract block votes.

As the wreckers moved in and many old watering holes were replaced with town house developments, some clubs survived by their ability to adapt and in being strategically located.

The Polish Club was an example.

The bar still was of dark wood, the room's panelled walls showed the arms of the Polish provinces and the national White Eagle on a red background held centre stage. A portrait of the late Pope John Paul II, once Archbishop of Krakow, gazed down from the entrance to the dining room.

But that was the extent of the ethnicity.

What northern European brews on offer were languishing dustily on side shelves behind the bar. Beer and wine and the expensive colourful cocktails young women liked were all Australian, as were the packaged crisps and peanuts encouraging thirst. The clientele was mixed and casually dressed, most were sitting on comfortable chairs around tables and as he made his way to Stan, Order overheard an animated conversation about mixed fortunes from the afternoon's seven race program at Canberra's track.

"Good to see you, John. What are you having?"

Stan was a big cuddly bear man, a director of the club and owner of a successful plumbing business. His antecedents went back to a grandfather who had worked on the Snowy.

Holding his own beer and Order's white wine, Stan led them further into the lounge to a table discretely out of earshot of other patrons.

"Got yourself a challenge, I hear," the big man said after they were seated. "Anything I can do to help?"

"Thanks, Stan. I think I can win."

"Of course you will. She'll be right." He silently toasted Order before drinking.

Wishing he hadn't used the popular but feminine term of reassurance, Order said: "There is something you could maybe help me with. I'm looking for someone."

He'd decided to tell Stan as little as possible about Mrs. Cohen's fears and the dead boy. He didn't think his friend was a gossip but it really didn't concern Stan and anyway, so far there was only a vague suspicion.

So Order fell back upon a common political stratagem.

"It's a constituent matter, Stan. I've been asked if I can track down an old friend of her daughter's. The girl's married an' living in the U.S.A. She's coming out on a quick visit an' asked if this friend was still around. It's a Polish name, so I thought you might be able to help."

"Do my best."

"It's K-o-r-z-e-n-i-o-w-s-k-i," Order spelled out, not prepared to trust his pronunciation. "Here, I've written it down."

Stan barely glanced at the paper.

"We haven't seen them around here for many many years, John. Too high an' mighty for us. An' why did she give you this name?" Stan's voice was gently reproving.

"It's not in the phone book," Order said lamely, as if this would justify his obvious blunder.

"Of course it isn't. The family hasn't used it for years," Stan said pointedly, increasing Order's discomfort. "Well before your constituent's daughter would have known them."

"I'd watch myself if I were you, John," Stan continued. "Whatever the reason, I don't think your woman is being honest with you and these are not people to trifle with."

"So who are they?" Order asked more confidently, now that the criticism for the clumsy deception was directed at his mythical constituent.

"They're the Conrad's, John. The jewellers. One of the biggest outfits on the east coast. Branches in Sydney, Melbourne, and Brisbane an' wherever an' still headquartered here. They live in a bloody great mansion in the diplomatic belt."

EIGHT

He had little time to consider the implications of Stan's identification, going from the club to a charity trivia night where his presence was publicly acknowledged and there was time to circulate among the other tables during the breaks between the rounds of questions.

It was good to be back mixing in the electorate after the trying week and although there were other politicians taking part the organisers paid him and his colleagues present the courtesy of only identifying them among the guests. Few actions irritated Order more at a function than an announcement of a list of apologies from members who were not there and, he suspected, never had intended to be.

As VIPs' the politicians were strategically seated throughout the room and Order was delighted when a weekly newspaper's photographer chose the table at which he was sitting for a social page item. He even remembered to follow Bernie's injunction never to be photographed with a glass in his hand. If you have one, the Party secretary had advised, and the balance of probabilities is that you will, hide it.

Bernie was held in awe and respect by the young and the new politicians. His time in the Party was legendary or as he put it: "I go back to the age of the great musicals like *Showboat* and *Carousel*, when you could understand the lyrics."

And this was the man he must consult before speaking again to Mrs. Cohen, Order realised late Sunday night, as he rested tired feet from an afternoon's doorknocking.

Not that he could do much immediately about the old lady, because Monday morning was Party meeting time and it was a sitting week.

When the parliament sat Party room debate was confined to the upcoming work of the House. The Opposition manager of business had a draft programme for the three days, listing legislation already introduced which was to be debated out, committee reports to be presented, government papers to be tabled, ministerial statements to be made and new legislation to be brought on.

The list was not detailed - no government would forewarn its opponents to that extent - nor was it comprehensive, items would be added and deleted as the sitting days progressed and circumstances demanded, but it was all the Opposition had to work from.

Notwithstanding the concentration upon the sitting the previous week's call for pre-selection candidates could not go unremarked and Fearless Leader made a brief general statement wishing well those under challenge. Order was comforted to note he was not alone, to judge from the gossip around him.

As the members talked through the meagre information they had at their disposal, allocating speakers and arguing tactics, Order appreciated if he lost out upon being selected how much he would miss the often chaotic, always tense, meetings in this crowded room.

There was nothing opulent about the surroundings, the legislature itself had not been in existence long enough to acquire the trappings of history.

A few original but indifferent art works sat high above, banished from the ministerial offices and corridors so rumour had it. A loose leaf set of the laws of the Australian Capital Territory and a complete set of parliamentary Hansard, the record of all debates in the House, placed within reachable distance along the walls added a practical touch. Several jugs of water and accompanying glasses completed the furnishings, apart from chairs.

And this was where it all happened.

You could forget the Chamber, because while the printed programme for the day seldom ran as planned - battle strategy rarely survives initial contact with the enemy - there was an ultimate predictability. With the Government and crossbench members outvoting them the Opposition simply had to accept the situation.

However in the Party room you could speak your mind, free from the pernicious and silencing effect of political correctness which made hypocrites of so many elected representatives in their public utterances. You could discuss openly the wildest of ideas, suggest outrageous plans to counter government moves or put forward crude manoeuvres to delay, perhaps even thwart, business, provided you could get the call to speak.

Seated comfortably toward the back of the room, buttressed by his friends Rob Glasson and Tim Forbes, Order could observe most of his parliamentary colleagues and he marvelled again how politics still was one of the few jobs where formal and now increasingly academic qualifications were not required.

This would change, he had no doubt. Some enterprising university would offer a full-blown degree in politics and some more human variety would be lost as members became clones of each other.

According to older representatives the rot already had set in. Recently Bob Buchan had lamented the passing of the parliamentary characters through death, defeat or retirement and their replacement by humourless zealots of both sexes.

As a relatively new boy, yet to face his first general election if he survived Lorraine Bennett's challenge, Order was in no position to judge the accuracy of this claim.

All he could see around him was a reasonable cross-section of a democratic society: the ambitious and the resigned, the drunks, the womanisers, the lazy and the industrious, the well-meaning and the ill-disposed, the slovenly and the dandies, the talkers and the doers.

Yet they all possessed one common link: they were here, they were winners.

"It's not Stalingrad legislation, y'know, to be fought over clause by clause," complained Paul Severin, who must have seen the film on the World War II battle currently screening.

"It's not 'til Thursday, Leader," explained Harrison 'Will' Ogilvie, the manager of Opposition business. "We could have our police committee have another look at it an' report back tomorrow."

"There goes lunch," muttered Tim Forbes, the Party's police spokesman, when Fearless Leader agreed. "You two will have to give my apologies."

"See you at the Convention Centre then, John," Rob Glasson confirmed, as they parted company in the corridor heading toward their offices.

"Okay," Order replied. Reminded by Severin's reference to World War II he had time to phone Bernie before the business lunch, which literally was within walking distance. Suburban Canberra might be expanding but the city retained a tight CBD.

It was a good lunch, a quarterly event which seldom failed to live up to culinary expectations. The table groupings were diplomatic, that is chosen with care, so there was not the slightest risk a party political argument could break out over the main course if someone had imbibed too many pre-lunch drinks.

Order dutifully listened to the talk of his host beside him - where you sat as an Opposition member often was indicative of the chances the organisers of such functions believed your party had to achieve government - and noted he and his colleagues now were moved up to the second line of tables, nearer the podium and the day's speaker.

The applause was generous, whether for the content of the speech or because it had concluded Order could not decide.

Because he was not listening.

"Conrad's. The jewellers," Bernie had confirmed earlier over the telephone. "Put a sparkle in your life, says the advertisement. Or still don't you watch television news, John?"

"No, I do, Bernie. I've just not seen what you're talking about."

Order did watch more television news now because he occasionally featured - like the preselection challenge, he thought bitterly. He'd even considered buying a video so if he missed the item by missing the news, he could view later to see how he performed. As Bernie had suggested.

"Difficult to miss if you're watching the news," Bernie observed dryly. "They only advertise in prime time."

In Order's silence, Bernie added: "They have a string of stores, retail outlets, along the eastern seaboard, not only in the major cities but also in regional centres. A private company, no listed shares on the Stock Exchange, I understand," Bernie qualified quickly, too quickly Order thought.

"I've not heard of them locally," he said slyly, remembering Stan's dismissive put-down.

"Not surprised," said Bernie, unflustered. "The Conrad's are national status. Refugee an' multicultural an' ethnic committee memberships. Chair of one, I think. The family is reputed to be close to the Prime Minister."

Order realised the lunch was concluded. People were rising from their seats, thanking their table host, bidding farewells and heading for the exit.

He dutifully and genuinely fulfilled these obligations, concentrating for the time it took to do so upon such courtesies, even remembering to leave his name tag which was now a dollar each to purchase he'd been told, and then returned to Bernie's concluding words.

"The Conrad's are very sympathetic to us, John. Very, very sympathetic. I've no doubt you'll be aware of this in whatever dealings you have with them."

NINE

He later wondered about the wisdom of seeing Mrs. Cohen immediately after the business luncheon. Although a moderate drinker and especially at public functions, Order was aware alcohol did loosen the tongue.

However he didn't have much choice in the timing of his visit. With the House sitting over the next three days there was no other opportunity except at inconvenient hours and he didn't want to keep an old lady waiting until Friday. The elderly, as he knew from other constituent dealings, fretted when they *were* kept waiting, probably because all time remaining to them was not to be wasted.

Mrs. Cohen had listened to him in silence, only nodding briefly when he mentioned the Korzeniowski to Conrad name change.

"It doesn't mean anything, Mrs. Cohen. Nothing definite that is."

"We've tracked down the person who killed Daniel Levy, Mr. Order."

"Now hold on. There's no proof."

"That's why he died. He found out his Australian identity," the old woman continued confidently, as if she hadn't heard him. "Now we must find out why it was necessary to kill him."

Unable to shake her conviction, Order promised to contact Mrs. Cohen again as soon - and if - he had more information and warned her that his next visit might be some time hence.

The Tuesday morning Party meeting was the usual mixture of

argument over tactics and reorganisation of speakers to accommodate the government's change of business on the daily programme.

While the speakers' list did not directly affect him, Order was instructed to perform House duty for the morning session.

It required no more than to be present in your seat until the lunch suspension and fulfilled no useful purpose as far as Order could understand other than to keep company the Opposition frontbench member who had charge of whatever legislation was being debated.

It was a quiet morning. The bill before the House was not contentious; however this did not reduce the amount of talk. Most politicians love the sound of their own voice and will draw out their speech to enjoy its Lorelei-like attraction.

Order had brought some papers from his office and was alternating between trying to concentrate upon their words and gazing achingly at the real world outside the glass doors of the public entrance, of which his seat in the parliament afforded him a narrow view, when Les Preen found him.

"Seen the paper?" he asked in a hushed voice, lest he incur the wrath of Deputy Speaker Burrows.

Preen was a plump, volatile gossip, intriguer and mischief maker. How he held his seat was a mystery if his constituents avoided him to the same overwhelming extent as did his colleagues.

Order saw the newspaper was the weekly for which he had been photographed at the Saturday trivia night for their social page.

He was reaching across to take it from Preen's hand and turn to the happy snap item when his colleague stopped him.

"No, there. The letter to the editor."

It was short and to the point. The writer was delighted Lorraine Bennett was standing for preselection because much needed to be done in the electorate, so neglected since the untimely death of Bevan Wilson.

"Ignore it, John," Liz advised him back in the office following the lunch suspension. "A government supporter being mischievous."

"Or one of ours supporting Lorraine. Do we know the name?"

"Not in the electoral roll or the phone book in that or any other of your suburbs."

"So probably used the maiden name," decided Order.

"No way can I reply," Order continued angrily. "There's nothing really to respond to. If I do reply an' list a lot of achievements, I'll look like I'm either trying to boost my preselection chances or I'm justifying myself - an' I don't think I have to."

All that bloody doorknocking, for this, he thought peevishly. Politics certainly wasn't for the thin skinned.

"And you might provoke more letters. People complaining about what you haven't done for them. Mrs. Boone an' her larger government house, for example."

"She's on the housing list, Liz. I'm not sure she even has time to read, from what I've seen of her family. So writing to the press is very unlikely."

"Just an example, John. What I'm saying is you don't want a public media brawl with the preselection coming up. Ignore it, you're the sitting member."

"When is preselection? Any news?"

"No. Look, why not think positive? Your newsletter's going out next week if we collect it from Rudi tomorrow. It will swamp a letter in a weekly throwaway lots of people don't read."

Let's hope it doesn't rain and swamp the newsletter too, he thought mournfully, not mollified by his secretary's encouragement.

Why was it politicians took any positive media as a small victory but something critical was their political ruin, Order wondered?

"And what is that?" he asked, noticing a large cardboard bin beside the office occasional table.

"It's a recycling box. Have you any idea how much paper comes through this place? I've been cleaning out your wastepaper basket for months."

"It can't stay there or here," Order said, indicating his office and petulantly exerting his authority after the embarrassing morale boost from his motherly secretary.

"Of course not. I wanted you to see it. It's going in my office. You've phone messages," she added, collecting the bin and leaving him alone.

Two pink slips of a message pad lay across his desk, a common enough event when he was absent in the House.

One was Preen, which he ignored, reasoning it was about the newspaper letter to judge by the time he'd phoned.

"Busy tonight?" asked Rabbit, when he responded to the second message.

Member's punctuality in attending the Chamber, despite the efforts of the whips, was very much determined by work there or the presence of the media. Question time immediately following the suspension for lunch however, always saw a full House. Noisy too, if like today the parliament was sitting after a two week break.

"Order! The House will come to order!" shouted Speaker Harris over the interjections and jeers of the Opposition to a rambling answer to Fearless Leader's first question.

While he shared the frustration of his colleagues at a minister replying to a question at length, as if the more words uttered would help clarify the matter, Order rarely joined in the raillery.

He knew it wasted precious time and he didn't want to further encourage the tiresome play upon his name that had dogged his first weeks in the parliament. But if asked he would not have given these as his prime reasons. Rather, he didn't find the interjections very funny, pithy or well targeted and knew he couldn't do any better.

Every now and then someone would take exception to a remark, because politicians are more sensitive to being misrepresented than a mole is to light.

Then the House would erupt, with both sides levelling points of order like mortar rounds to break up their opponent's attack and force a withdrawal of the inflammatory comment.

With tempers running hot this was the danger time, when an ill-chosen word and a stubborn adherence to its accuracy could see a member suspended.

Yet even this ultimate punishment was not prolonged because any animosity was not personal. Members knew they could not afford to carry a grudge; they had to sit in committee with someone they'd been verbally fighting across the floor or needed support from for a matter in the House.

Some were personal friends off the carpet and while this fraternisation was discouraged by the diehards, it was a truism your real political enemies often were in your own ranks. Julie Davenport, for example, thought Order as Speaker Harris with visible relief called for parliamentary papers to be presented.

Another question time had been negotiated with minimum disruption and nobody had been tossed out.

Bored with the tabling of Government reports and the Opposition's adjournment of debate upon them, Order returned to his office.

En route on the stairs he encountered Edward 'Teddy' Beare, a government backbencher.

"Preselection challenge, John. How does it look?"

"I should be okay," Order said guardedly, with more confidence than he felt, and defensively returned the question: "How's Craddock doing? "

"We haven't called for nominations yet." Not unfriendly but equally cautious, then Beare added: "Good luck."

Continuing his climb Order realised how difficult it was to dislike individual politicians and if you did, you could try only to avoid them.

TEN

It was a risk organising any activity for the evening of a parliamentary sitting day: it simply couldn't be predicted if the House would rise early or late.

A minor debate suddenly would take off, the more speakers joining in encouraging others to participate, also compelled to get their remarks into the record.

As the hands of the clocks around the Chamber approached five thirty, the Government and Opposition Whips held quiet conversations together and with the smaller party crossbenches and independent members. How long would this debate last? Who else wanted to speak? What other business did the House want to deal with today? Could they complete it all by seven o'clock and adjourn or would they suspend for a compulsory dinner break? And if they were to sit after dinner, how many Opposition pairs had to be negotiated for ministers - any backbenchers' arrangements were irrelevant - with prior commitments for the evening?

There was only one certainty if the legislature sat after a dinner recess: the House would make a night of it. No going home half an hour after resuming, because no member wanted their cancelled plans wasted. Perversely, the members would make each other pay for the collective talkativeness of the day.

Order was lucky. There was an important black tie tourism function that evening demanding the presence of senior parliamentarians from all parties and agreement was reached for a six-thirty adjournment by postponing several items upon the daily programme until later in the week.

He'd phoned Rabbit when he again returned to his now empty office - Liz didn't work evenings - after the House had risen and arranged to meet her in an hour at his flat.

He still was enjoying the simple uncomplicated lust of the affair but the need for secrecy was creating increased difficulties. Even the end of daylight saving was not the blessing he had hoped for.

Granted, it was dark now when they met but the risk remained of his car parked outside or too close to her suburban house being noticed the more frequent the visits.

His flat was anonymous, the building's car park the scene of constant comings and goings and, he suspected, the other residents attitudes to affairs considerably more relaxed than the occupants of suburban quarter acre blocks in good neighbourhoods. The pad was not as comfortable as Rabbit's home, but what really was necessary for a sexual tryst?

The pre-selection threat had further complicated the relationship. Wednesday had been no last fling, nothing had been resolved and he couldn't see an immediate way out, even if he'd wanted to end the association.

"You've been in the news, John," she murmured later. "Another woman. Though she's after your seat," and chuckled.

Order stroked the back of her head, snuggled into his neck.

"Nothing I can't handle."

"I'm sure. Can I help?"

"You are already," he assured her, but the warning bells were ringing.

"No, in other ways," Rabbit's hand stroked his chest. "If you're not elected, what would you do? Leave Canberra?"

"No way. It's not going to happen. I'll win the pre-selection." He transferred a hand to beneath the doona. "Don't worry about it. Let's concentrate on the here an' now."

"Let's," Rabbit moved co-operatively. "I don't want to lose you, that's all, John."

After she had gone home Order weighed up his situation. He hoped he'd sounded both confident and sincere, even if he was neither.

If he was defeated by Lorraine Bennett he'd be out of this relationship and its implication of getting serious, because there was no point in staying in Canberra.

Work was difficult to find for a losing politician. You were tainted. Half of the city's employers would not give you a job because they disagreed with political affiliations and the other half because while sympathetic to your politics, they did not want it known so openly. The apolitical public service was out and your chance of scoring a government appointment to one of the many commissions or boards was dependent upon *your* side being in government and also being favourably disposed toward *you*. As a first time then unsuccessful parliamentarian, a oncer, Order did not rate himself highly in the preferment stakes.

The best he could hope for was being taken onto the staff of another successful candidate, which was back where he had started.

It was not an appealing prospect.

He didn't want the pitying generosity of one of his current peers and he knew he could not tolerate the daily humiliation of Lorraine Bennett occupying his parliamentary seat.

So goodbye Rabbit and goodbye Canberra.

And it might come to that anyway, recalling Bernie's warning about the power the man exerted and Marek Conrad's own telephone call during the afternoon.

Order again had been clearing his desk. The usual untidy floor heap of magazines, brochures, newsletters and other debris from around the country which all politicians received freely and unsolicited and destined for the new recycling box, his eyes keeping up with the televised debate and the movement of the whips around the Chamber.

Liz had put him through and the man, after a brief introduction, continued: "A Mrs. Cohen spoke to me today. We need to talk. Ten o'clock, my office."

"We're sitting at ten-thirty, Mr. Conrad," replied Order, anger rising at the blunt command.

"Nine then. I'm going to Melbourne. Twelfth floor, Kingston Business Centre." Authoritatively and the line was disconnected.

Typical that the bastard was on the top floor was all Order could think.

ELEVEN

Conrad's was not only on the top floor, it *was* the top floor of one of Canberra's newest and most controversial buildings.

Development controversy was usual in this city. Hardly was the turning of a sod proposed without bringing forth protests of one sort or another. If it was a green field site the environmentalists would be complaining, if redevelopment of an existing block the heritage forces would be grumbling.

So there were dark rumours about how this tall oblong of glass and steel had managed to circumvent Canberra's strict building height laws to command a magnificent view of Lake Burley Griffin over the smart Kingston Foreshores residential area and Marek Conrad had primacy even of this scene.

Order had no time to fully appreciate the expansive backdrop.

Marek Conrad sat facing his guest behind a large varnished wooden desk with a leather top and drawers with brass handles. The room was fitted out in a similar heavy old-fashioned style, several glass bookcases, and an ornate hat stand. Order recognised the re-conditioned surplus furniture from Old Parliament House, which had been vacated in 1988.

Conrad himself was of average height and heavy set, probably the result of adherence to a northern European diet, Order decided. His face was round and with a fashionably shaved head and open neck shirt, he didn't look much like a successful businessman.

His behaviour belied the aggressive telephone approach. Gone was yesterday's abruptness.

"Thank you for coming at such short notice, Mr. Order," he began. "Can I offer you coffee?"

"No thanks." Order was still defensive.

"Your friend Mrs. Cohen phoned yesterday about an accidental death last week," the middle-aged man continued, "except she didn't think it was an accident."

Order remained silent.

"She made some wild accusations, libellous in fact, and gave you as the source for contacting me." He stared disapprovingly at his guest.

"She was looking for someone of Polish extraction. I found the name you had changed to and told my *constituent*." Order stressed the word. "Whatever else she may have said was her own invention."

"I'm glad to hear it. My family has been here in Canberra a very long time. Well over sixty years. We've been successful and have built up a reputation for probity in our dealings - both in and out of business. Naturally we would not want, nor take kindly to, unsubstantiated allegations, even made by an old lady."

Order again remained silent.

"Mrs. Cohen seemed to believe I had something to do with this man's fatal accident. In fact she said he had a meeting with me that night at his hotel."

Did you, Order was tempted to ask, but confined himself to a neutral: "That's what she said?"

"Yes. I gathered she'd discussed these silly ideas with you, Mr. Order. Preposterous, of course," Marek Conrad was pleased to have drawn another response, however cautious. "But do you believe her, Mr. Order?"

"I don't believe anything, Mr. Conrad," he said carefully. "I simply helped resolve a constituent's enquiry."

"Would you have done so if you'd known where it would lead?"

The injured persuasive tone had developed an edge of anger.

"Well, would you?"

Order fought to control his own temper. You're not taking to a salesgirl who just botched a deal, mate. No third degree here.

"Probably not. I certainly didn't know she would contact you."

"Probably not," the jewellery king mimicked. "D'you always hand out highly private information so gratuitously?"

"I help my constituents to the best of my ability, Mr. Conrad," Order said honestly. "Like most people they don't always behave sensibly." Then he added: "Sometimes they do very stupid things."

Conrad's reaction surprised him. Here they were in the preliminaries of a verbal brawl then the man leaned back and smiled.

"You're right, of course. You've a difficult job to do, Mr. Order. Even more difficult now, I understand, and you meet a far wider cross-section of people than I do. Forgive my irritableness but I don't want this absurd suggestion to gain credence."

"You'd like me to talk to Mrs. Cohen?"

"I would. Set her mind at rest that I had nothing, absolutely nothing, to do with this unfortunate young man's death."

"Okay. I'll do my best." Impressed with the man's sincerity.

"Thank you. I really appreciate your help. If I can ever return the favour. We're not without -"

"Thanks, Mr. Conrad, but I'll win."

"I don't doubt it." Conrad stood, came around the desk and shook Order's hand. "Still, if there's anything…" He led the way from the room.

Conrad paused at his office door.

"Did Mrs. Cohen mention to you any papers she had?"

"No, she didn't. Why?"

"She mentioned some to me. See if you can find out, would you? It might help clear up the misunderstanding. I'm sure there are other Korzeniowski's around."

"But not this one," Order said affably.

The smile was immediate.

"No, not this one, Mr. Order."

* * *

"Sorry," he mouthed to a disapproving Harold Chambers as he slipped late into the Party room meeting. The Whip's expression did not alter and Order wondered if there was more boring House duty in store, a favourite punishment for infringements.

"Tomorrow afternoon the education amendments are being brought on," the business manager, Ogilvie, confirmed with his slight Scots accent. "We have some of our own, don't we?"

"Mandatory voluntary contributions," said Eric White, the education spokesman.

"Contradiction in terms," interjected Paul Severin.

"You know what I mean, Paul," said White wearily, having heard the same comment ever since the Party had decided to proceed with the policy.

"It won't get up," Julie Davenport, an original opponent, said dogmatically.

"Tactics, Julie. We owe it to our school constituency," White countered.

Voluntary fees raised strong passions.

Nobody doubted schools needed more money but whereas the opponents of the levy argued education was theoretically free and any shortfall therefore should be made up by government funding, the realists accepted that because this would never happen, parents however reluctantly must make up the difference in the interests of their children's education.

The dispute was clouded by claims many parents who took the voluntary term literally were those who could afford to pay and did not, while the financially strapped made great sacrifices to meet the unenforceable charge.

"We'll need a full team. You Julie an' John. John? John Order, wherever you are," called White.

Julie Davenport and John Order were the Opposition's members of the parliament's Education Committee. Normally comprising five people so the government had the numbers, the committee recently had expanded to six to accommodate crossbench representation. This even number should have given the Opposition the chance occasionally to hang a vote three all, but as they knew by experience the sixth member's debt for inclusion was unfailing support for the status quo.

Order waved his hand as present and Fearless Leader reminded the Party room their position upon voluntary fees was policy, thus endorsing the unwinnable amendment.

Ogilvie moved to the next item on the notice paper and Eric White scuttled back to where Order was sitting just inside the door.

"Did you hear all that?" he asked softly and when Order nodded White added, almost silently mouthing the words: "You speak third for us. Take up what she misses, deliberately or otherwise. Julie's unreliable."

You can say that again, thought Order, half expecting to see Lorraine Bennett present in the strictly members only Party room deliberations.

White waylaid him again later as the meeting concluded, but not before Harold Chambers told him he would be asking a question today.

"Not that you deserve it," the old Whip said, his bald head reflecting the corridor lighting.

"Sorry, Harold. I - well, something important came up."

"You're not married, so your wife didn't die, Order." For some reason Chambers always addressed people by their last name, a regression to the business world of the fifties, like ties, suits and discipline. "Can't think of any other reason to be late for the *regular* Party meeting."

Order's repeat apologies were lost with Eric White's intervention.

"Need to see you and Julie here," he gave an unconvincing smile to the woman beside him, "sometime to work out tactics for tomorrow."

"Tactics!" Julie Davenport sniffed.

"I know your bloody views, Julie. An' you know the Party line. Now, when do we meet?"

It was an odd arrangement, Opposition frontbenchers not being on the parliamentary committees their portfolio responsibilities shadowed in the House.

"Makes sense though, John," his friend, Rob Glasson, had explained early in Order's career as a politician. "Stops the Party getting locked into a committee decision by majority vote. Our spokesman," Glasson too didn't believe in political correctness, "therefore isn't bound by it."

"What about our own committee members? If they go along with the majority of the committee an' our spokesman won't support the decision, they'll look stupid."

"So know Party policy. You're not on a committee to make up the numbers."

"What if the Party doesn't have a policy?"

"Then talk to our official spokesman. You're on education, right? Then it's Eric White."

"Not this Julie Davenport? I'm on the committee with her."

In those early days Order, the by-election winner, found himself courted by parliamentary Party members who hoped to bring him into their faction: the dries or the wets. He'd been surprised to discover such groupings existed, unbeknown to all but the most senior of the Party's rank and file supporters.

They were drinking coffee in a secluded part of the almost empty parliamentary dining room. Nevertheless Rob Glasson said quietly: "Talk to Eric."

And seeing Order's doubt, Glasson relaxed and grinned.

"John, you'll find your committee colleagues friendly and companionable, as it should be because you have to work with them and possibly travel interstate also, on committee enquiries. But don't be fooled. They have their hard line political beliefs an' they'll promote them."

Because Order still looked confused, Glasson added: "I repeat, the committee will be very friendly, particularly the Chair, because he'll be trying to get you on side."

"I've got to work with them, Rob." Order's tone turned to despair.

"Of course. Just remember, they're all bastards. Political opponents. But they're also human. A committee is like the House itself. You can hate them all, then someone tells a joke or there's a request for a pair because of a sick child -"

"This absence of policy worries me. How do I know what to do? Julie Davenport's been on education since the election, shouldn't I consult her?"

"Talk to Eric," Glasson repeated cautiously. "Julie's views might not conform to your own - or Eric's."

"But then we'll have an Opposition split."

"No we won't. Eric calls the shots in education policy. You two do as he says."

"But committee reports are under embargo until tabled in the House."

"You must talk to, well, Eric in this case, *before* the report is agreed to by the committee. It's okay to talk to our spokesman about the general thrust or direction of a report, but there is no point in doing so after the committee has unanimously agreed to it. If you agreed an' then for whatever reason subsequently dissent, you'll lose credibility with everyone - an' I mean everyone - in the parliament."

TWELVE

Order remembered the long ago conversation, barely twelve months really, as he sat in Eric White's crowded office.

It was, to his tidy mind, an indescribable jumble of papers. The man mustn't throw anything away.

Spare chairs, the occasional table, the desk and surrounding floor, were stacked with heaps of reports, newspapers and magazines, as was the window ledge and the bookcases behind were White now sat, coincidentally recalling the topic of Order's conversation with Glasson.

"But we didn't dissent," Julie Davenport was pleading, to her obvious discomfort. "The committee report said voluntary should stay voluntary."

"I know," said White, patting a pile of papers beside him. "You should have an' now you'll have to cop any flak when I move our amendment tomorrow."

White's smile was thin and humourless.

"Now, if you'll excuse me …"

"Policy change, perhaps, Eric?" Davenport ventured, desperate to avoid the indignity of being criticised in the debate.

"No. There's been no change to policy an' I'm not having our clear position appear unclear because you stuffed up."

"Electoral consultations maybe?" Order suggested.

"That's more like it," White agreed. "Yes. You two can say since the report was tabled you've spoken more widely in the community and formed the view your original agreement to the recommendation was wrong. Oppositions always consult with the electorate, governments don't have time. Everybody knows that so you'll probably get away with it."

"But it means saying we were wrong," Julie Davenport said heatedly.

"Take it or leave it, Julie, an' remember, a person who never apologizes is not at peace with themselves."

Eric's becoming quite a philosopher, thought Order, then the education spokesman added: "I'd say you owe our newest member here, for getting you both off the hook."

Which was what I didn't need, Order decided, hurrying back to his office. Putting her in his debt had humiliated Julie Davenport and politicians rarely forgot such incidents. He realised too the woman had neither addressed nor looked at him during their time with White.

"Newsletter won't be ready today," Liz announced as he was removing his coat. "Machine's playing up, but Rudi swears it will be available for pick-up lunchtime tomorrow."

"We time to make this weekend's walkers?"

Like some other politicians and many retail businesses, Order relied upon a company with a force of casual employees, or walkers, to deliver his quarterly electoral newsletter.

"Five o'clock tomorrow's the deadline."

"Arnie's van still available?"

"I'll reconfirm."

"I'd like to get the message out a.s.a.p., Liz. The further into autumn, the more chance of rain an' nobody wants to read an electoral report that's been half sticking from a letterbox in a thunderstorm."

"Tell them to put it right inside the box."

"Every time."

They both knew the futility of the request.

The walkers were either young children, often trailed by mum in the family car, encouraged by their parents to earn money to buy a bike, a surfboard or whatever, or they were overseas immigrants looking to supplement their income with part-time work. Payment was by article so only four or five items bundled together made the job marginally viable and the niceties of letterboxing such a bulky delivery were forgotten in the rush to cover the designated area on time.

"The no junk mail?" Liz asked tentatively.

It was a debate which never ended.

Discussed in every parliament from whence newsletters, how-to-votes, electoral pamphlets and the like were distributed to constituent's letterboxes without the authoritative stamp of the official postal service: do you or don't you put the aforesaid items in mailboxes with no junk mail or similarly worded signs to discourage advertising brochures?

Those who believed you could do so argued whatever message they were delivering to their constituents under no circumstances could or should be considered as junk mail. Those less self-opinionated pointed out that that assumption depended upon the person receiving the information, not the person providing it.

There always were complaints, particularly during election campaigns, however most politicians ignored them, taking comfort from the belief the only people who did object weren't going to vote for you anyway, so who cared what they thought.

Unless you held a narrow 176 vote majority from a by-election win twelve months ago.

Order knew the arguments. He also knew in the up-market areas of his electorate where some preselection voting members lived there were many more no junk mailboxes than in the poorer parts of the constituency. People on low incomes could not afford to risk missing an advertised bargain or sale letterboxed to their homes.

"I can't take the chance, Liz. It's going to be a tight fight with

Lorraine Bennett an' I daren't offend a preselection voter over a no junk issue. The newsletter's important to the campaign 'though. Show's the branch members I'm out there working. Any ideas?"

"Why not post them? We've the voting membership list."

"Jayson's in?"

Liz nodded. "Out to lunch."

"Get him to check out our members in the up-market areas for no junk signs. We can map a route. In fact he could do the lot. How many d'you reckon can vote?"

"Fifty four."

"The lot then. The electoral allowance can stand the postage. We can work on it this afternoon."

"Not we, me. You've got House duty from question time until adjournment or suspension for dinner."

Bastard. The Whip's punishment for arriving late to the Party meeting.

There was a rumour Wendy Wonder, aka Wendy the Wonder Woman or VW – WWW, three W's – was after Harold Chamber's job. Feisty, argumentative, bossy, Order almost was prepared to vote for her if she challenged the old disciplinarian.

"Sorry, didn't catch that," he apologised.

"Jayson needs transport."

"Of course." Order didn't know if Jayson had wheels, as his generation would have said, but in any case he couldn't be expected to use his own vehicle and petrol for Order's preselection campaigning.

"He can use my car this afternoon while I'm on House penance. Shouldn't take too long if it's properly planned. Just mark the no junk letterboxes on our membership list an' be back by five-thirty, okay?"

As Liz was leaving his office a difficulty occurred to Order.

"Jayson has permission to drive my car, hasn't he, Liz?"

"He has, John. I organised it when he joined us."

"Tell him it's Canberra not Le Mans," Order instructed, aware a six cylinder Camry might prove a greater temptation for an impecunious uni student to floor than any nubile female co-ed.

Liz again had turned away when Order said: "I'm to ask a question. Has it shown up yet?"

"Not yet."

Most other backbenchers shared his dislike of asking questions prepared by backroom boffins, who worked in such closeted environments they knew little of the real world of politics.

Too often their questions were unclear or verbose or both. Worse, the members who were instructed to ask the questions often themselves did not understand what answers they were seeking. Thus they lacked confidence in the delivery.

And it showed.

Sharing the impatient opportunism of any newly elected member to bask in the light of publicity, Order much preferred to ask a populist question, ideally relating to his own electorate. Say a specific school's problem with maintenance or, if this was not possible, then a general question about school maintenance across Canberra.

Such opportunities did not occur often and having been embarrassed on several occasions by obviously not knowing what he was talking about when asking a prepared question, Order wanted any boffin's offering as early as possible. That way he could acquaint himself and become comfortable with what he had to ask.

"And Liz ..."

His secretary again checked her departure.

"Any news on the preselection date?"

"Not yet," Liz said with a touch of weariness and then: "Ah, the question. Thanks, Clare."

Clare, the tall willowy blonde who worked for Fearless Leader. The young woman his parliamentary colleague Brian was alleged to be pining for.

Poor Brian's sexual fantasies were forgotten when Order read the question. Incomprehensible was the word which came quickest to mind. He angrily punched the telephone buttons.

"What the Hell does this mean?"

"Who is speaking please?" The unmistakable voice, in deference to multiculturalism, of the new Asian staffer in Fearless Leader's office.

"Order. Where's Selby?"

"Miss Selby is at lunch. Who is speaking please?"

"Ask her to telephone John Order urgently," he said slowly, trying to keep his temper under control until, having repeated the message a third time, he replaced the receiver abruptly.

"Liz," he said over the intercom, "if ever Selby gets my message, ask her to provide an urgent brief on this bloody financial question." Otherwise I'm going to have to put in an Academy Award performance when asking it, he decided.

And why does every organisation put people who do not fully understand English onto answering telephones? he asked himself.

"Sorry, Liz, what was that?"

"Mrs. Cohen wants to see you tomorrow. She rang while you were on the phone. I explained the House was sitting and suggested one o'clock."

"There's the newsletter to be collected."

"You can do both in two hours. " This was the generous lunch suspension.

"Okay. " I do need to see her, Order admitted guiltily.

THIRTEEN

Why do tabling speeches need to be read, Order wondered? And why are they so often so long? A frustrated speechwriter perhaps, trapped in the sober attire of a pedantic government legislative draughtsman?

It wasn't as if the parliaments' of today were filled with illiterates, everyone could read, so the minute detail of every piece of new legislation being introduced did not have to be spelled out.

Nobody listened anyway. Even those who had responsibility for the opposition or crossbench response would not be relying upon some minister's bored monologue to shape their advice to colleagues and comments to the public. They'd carefully read for themselves the statement and the accompanying explanatory memorandum.

"Mr. Keane," intoned the Speaker, as the Minister concluded.

"Mr. Speaker, I move the debate be adjourned," said the Opposition's business spokesman.

"The question is the debate be adjourned and the adjourned debate be made an order of the day for the next sitting? Those of that opinion say Aye, contrary No? The Ayes have it. Minister?"

Order again wondered if Speaker Harris deliberately quoted the whole formal rigmarole without drawing breath just to lighten the tedium. Keane already had departed the Chamber, the Clerk was announcing the next Bill, the Opposition spokesman was present and the next Minister was poised to rise and deliver another turgid tabling speech.

Order recalled Party room discussions about the need for flex-ibility in parliamentary procedures and the virtual impossibility of actually changing the traditions and forms of the House and its Standing Orders. The latter a monolithic and cumbersome maze of regulations set in centuries old history, which was zealously protected by the staff of the parliament, principal among whom where the Clerks.

If, as occasionally happened, there was a break with tradition, like the decision years before to allow breastfeeding on the floor of the House, these guardians' acquiesced without argument to the amendment to standing orders.

With their long experience, they knew what was possible and what was not. How many female politicians just to make a statement, which may or may not be supported by their constituency voters, wanted every man in the Chamber perving on their breasts?

Not that Order could see any female around him he'd want to see breastfeeding anywhere.

He had been saved at question time from asking Selby's in-comprehensible question, not because she had got back to him, she hadn't, but because the strict forty-five minutes for questions without notice had run out before he was recognised.

Longwinded answers from ministers were a ploy used to take up time. Although the rules required replies to be concise and relevant to the question asked, these limitations still gave an experienced minister ample scope to drag out a response.

The manoeuvre also presented the Opposition strategists with the dilemma of taking points of order about the length and the relevance of the reply, thus using up more time, or allowing the minister to prolong the answer, which had the same result.

The more experienced ministers were adept at spinning out their replies, especially to a Dorothy Dix - a question asked by one of their own backbench members to allow ministers to publicise government achievements - and took full advantage of these opportunities, as if frequent flyer points were earned for every word uttered.

Anyway, he'd been saved. Selby's unasked question returned to her armory, perhaps to be asked tomorrow or not at all.

And whether he would ask a question the next day was not guaranteed, in spite of a roster which ostensibly carried over your chance if you missed out. Like the weather topical political issues were unpredictable and, if important enough, your place would be taken by a frontbencher in order to capitalise upon the current climate.

Since question time concluded and the Chamber emptied of most members, Order had been trying to establish how many others were left here on penance duty. Finn was the only member on his side of the House consistently in attendance, but Finlay usually dozed off after lunch wherever he was, so his presence signified nothing.

Others were coming and going as the business before the parliament dictated and Jenny Fellows was their frontbench minder.

Seeing the plump homely woman who seemed to be everyone's friend and who handled welfare issues for the Party, Order speculated what had caused her to become a politician.

He doubted it was ambition. Motherly Jenny showed none of the quiet ruthlessness which belonged to those with that aim. Nor was she a publicity junkie, complaining about being ignored by the media - the withdrawal symptoms of a news seeking addict - if she failed to feature over any forty- eight hour period. And she didn't power dress: a constantly changing wardrobe of bright colours, reds and yellows preferred, guaranteed to attract attention like a sports car to a police motorcyclist.

Jenny Fellows appointment to the Opposition frontbench had led to brief and at the time intense speculation.

Order's two close friends held differing opinions, neither flattering in this world of inflated egos.

Rob Glasson believed she was ambitious and masked it better than most, while Tim Forbes thought the promotion simply was a smart tactical move.

"She's harmless, so she's no threat to anyone else, unlike a few others we know. An' the welfare portfolio's made for her. She's so caring. She oozes commitment. Just the person to deal with those demanding community groups. A sympathetic ear an' a big enough shoulder to cry on."

Of the two, Order inclined to Forbes view now, as he suspected did most other members. Certainly there was no more speculation and no criticism either.

Watching the welfare spokeswoman making notes as the Minister uttered supportive words but promised nothing in reply to a crossbench suggestion, Order decided Jenny Fellows was a rare breed of politician whose new member enthusiasm to help humanity survives the cynical realities of prolonged political life.

Somehow she had retained untarnished the innocent zeal. Knee deep in the problems of the poor, the sick, the inept, of youth refuges and of quasi-job substitution schemes, all of which often seemed no more than giving hope to society and concerned parents.

And the daily frustrations of battling a government or an underclass which too often was incapable of doing the right thing for itself. Welfare isn't about successes, John, he recalled Bernie telling him early in his political career, it's about harm minimisation. Ours.

Order had decided some time ago Jenny Fellows was a saint and the Opposition was lucky to have her.

His attitude was biased, he realised. Jenny Fellows was an older post-children version of his ex-wife. Jan would have been this plump satisfied mother now, just as she had wanted before his ambition had demanded caution before the enormous responsibility of a family led to the divorce. He hadn't seen her for a long time. Didn't even know where she was.

The note was delivered by Jack, an attendant who had been working in the House longer than the parliament itself, it was claimed.

Saturday, 5 April. Preselection, he read in his secretary's sprawling handwriting. A telephone number was added and the word: *Urgent*.

"Finn? Finn, wake up!" The man gazed at him blearily. "Can you cover house duty for me? House duty? I've an urgent call to make."

Probably thinks I've gone to the toilet, he thought, hurrying into the fortuitously deserted Opposition lobby.

"John? Thank God you've rung. I must see you urgently."

"Rabbit! Everything alright? You haven't had an accident?"

"You could say that, I suppose. I might be pregnant."

FOURTEEN

It had the makings of a lousy evening.

The adjournment debate dragged on, with members who hadn't shown their faces in the Chamber all day save for the compulsory Question Time, now springing to their feet to claim the next five minutes to praise some obscure local activity in their electorate.

It was, Order knew because he occasionally had used the opportunity himself, a chance to ingratiate yourself with a few voters. The media, of course, never reported such blatant self-advertising exercises, but if you photocopied your Hansard remarks and posted them to the constituents involved …

He'd been tempted to cancel the school awards night he'd accepted in view of Rabbit's crisis call, until he recalled Bernie's thoughtful advice.

"You must remember," the old Party secretary had said through a cloud of smoke, "what's just another function to you is often the highlight of the year and the conclusion to weeks of work for the organisers. Never belittle them for their efforts."

And as he drove to the school Order also remembered Bernie's concluding remark: it's better not to go at all than to be a bad guest.

Well, he had attended and he had not been a bad guest. A little late, granted, thanks to the adjournment talkers, and a little stressed by arriving later than planned.

Nevertheless he had been warmly welcomed and publicly acknowledged. Because it was a primary school activity the formal evening was over by eight-thirty, allowing Order to excuse himself due to another electoral commitment from the lamingtons, sandwiches and sausage rolls supper

It was dark, it was cold and he parked in the driveway.

Rabbit couldn't be sure she was pregnant. Some irregularity was not uncommon. Yes, she had been a little uptight lately, through work she was quick to add, to Order's silent relief.

Her initial slightly tearful concern - she looked as if she'd been crying earlier - settled down under this patient questioning.

Now for the big one.

From behind his coffee cup Order asked: "An' you an' David?"

"Of course. We're not estranged. Or only during the week. I thought the same thing." Rabbit grinned. "Though' you and I are more regular - and unrestrained."

Which they had been immediately.

In for a penny, Order decided as he drove home, feeling a little guilty.

Still, if you accepted the massive difficulty of having any life other than politics, then why bother? You might as well simply give in and lose your real self. He understood, without sympathy, his poor besotted parliamentary colleague, Brian.

Except that his political future could hang upon Rabbit's condition.

No friendly voter, he knew, gave their Member anything but total loyalty and were tolerant of most foibles, save fraud and child abuse, but mucking around with an absent husband's wife would not enhance his preselection chances. Rabbit had promised to let him know when she was sure one way or the other. If the other it would have to be suppressed until after preselection.

What would happen then he was prepared to leave for now. Meantime, small mercies, Lorraine Bennett hadn't white-anted him at the school awards night.

Thursday morning the pluses and minuses of yesterday were behind him, as was the Party room meeting.

"Look's like I've missed out on a question today, Liz. The political caravan's moved on." Or Selby and her experts had scanned the morning newspaper for topical issues: always a dumb move because the Government's minders also could read and prepared answers just in case.

"You've Mrs. Cohen to see and the newsletter to collect in the lunch break and the education debate this afternoon."

"I hear you. I'll ring Gabby Williams then I'll work on education. Close off the phone would you, Liz." Order paused, remembering last night's promise. "Unless it's urgent, of course."

"Of course." Was there a cheeky tone, he wondered?

"No news from Tel Aviv, John."

"Bit slow, aren't they?"

"I can't say. There are more suicide bombings in Israel an' a tourist bus has crashed on the way to Egypt, injuring some Australians - it's in the paper. I guess our diplomatic representatives have other things to do." For the laconic Detective Inspector Williams it was a speech.

"Okay. Sorry, Gabby. I'm seeing Mrs. Cohen at lunchtime, so I thought I'd check with you first." Order realised, probably after the apology, he'd been speaking to a dead telephone.

His penalty to the Whip paid off, Order worked on his contribution to the education debate, glancing occasionally at the autumnal downpour thundering past the window, while in the House the government's executive business was introduced.

By the lunch suspension the rain had gone, leaving behind steaming streets, pooled water and, as he drew closer to Mrs. Cohen's house, increasing accumulations of fallen leaves.

He had not bothered to phone ahead. Old as she was, Lydia Cohen, as time had shown, was not forgetful and elderly people usually looked forward to a visitor.

Which was why he was worried when his third knock on the door and fourth ring of the bell still went unanswered.

An elderly neighbour was trundling his wheelie bin back onto his property from the curb side collection point.

"Can't help you," he replied to the question, his eyes trying to identify Order. "Don't know her."

A common difficulty in a growing city. "Anyone who might?"

"Try across the street. I've seen her talking to Mrs. Bennett. She'll know. Makes it her business to," he muttered, turning away.

That bloody name again, Order cursed, as he moved toward the guvvie, noting uneasily Mrs. Cohen's emptied garbage bin still sat on the nature strip.

"Lydia?" Mrs. Bennett was a spritely old lady who opened the door before he knocked. "No, I haven't seen her today. I hope nothing's wrong."

"So do I, Mrs. Bennett. I have an appointment with her an' there's no answer when I knock."

Mrs. Bennett, following Neighbourhood Watch instructions, glanced again from his business card to his face.

"Now I know you. You're Mr. Order, the politician."

"That's right, Mrs. Bennett," he said with great patience and some pleasure.

"Perhaps we should see if Lydia's alright. She has a heart condition, you know."

"Yes, I do know. But I can't get into the house."

"Oh I've got a key," Mrs. Bennett volunteered brightly. "I'll just go and get it, it's in my handbag."

Mrs. Cohen lay sprawled face down on the living room floor beside the occasional table, now askew, and surrounded by what must have been her heart tablets.

"She's alive. Unconscious but alive," said a suddenly invigorated Mrs. Bennett from beside the body. "You've a telephone? Then phone an ambulance," she added, when Order nodded.

Mrs. Bennett went further into the house, returning with a bowl of water and a box of tissues.

"Look's like she hit her head when she fell," she explained, dabbing a gash on the side of Mrs. Cohen's forehead, something Order had not noticed.

"She going to be okay?" Order watched the capable hands.

"Should be. Hasn't been here long, I'd say. Hospital for observation, of course. I'm a retired nurse, Mr. Order," by way of explanation.

The ambulance arrived; the officers came in, examined the patient and went back for the trolley. Mrs. Bennett's prediction proving correct she went off for the clothes and paraphernalia old lady's need in hospital while Order stood around uselessly.

"We'll need to go with her, Mr. Order," the retired nurse said companionably. "Do the paperwork. She's all alone. I'm probably her closest friend but I don't have a car."

"Liz? There's been an accident. We're taking Mrs. Cohen to hospital. No, I'll explain later. Tell Rudi I can't collect the newsletter today an' tell Arnie thanks but I don't need his panel van yet. Yes, next week now, so it's closer to the preselection."

"What?"

"The ambulance is about to leave. I can't guarantee when I'll be back. Tell Chambers, please. I don't know," distractedly, as the trolley moved carefully through the front door. "Get Bob Buchan to take my place in the debate - or Clarrie Evans, he can talk on anything," and usually does, Order thought. "I've got to go, Liz. I'll get back to you."

"Nasty cut on Lydia's forehead, Mr. Order," said Mrs. Bennett, after she had complimented him on the car, as he drove carefully following the ambulance. "Those table's have such sharp edges. Manufacturers' should be made to take more care."

Order murmured his agreement, but he wondered.

"You think she fell earlier today, Mrs. Bennett?"

"Oh yes," she said confidently, sitting up straight in her seat clutching her handbag and enjoying the drive.

"Then it's a good thing we found her so soon." He paused. "She didn't have any other visitors this morning?"

"Not that I saw, although I wasn't looking, of course. But I wouldn't know anyway, with the thunderstorm you couldn't see a hand in front of your face. Absolutely black, it was."

FIFTEEN

"**H**arold Chambers was very decent about it, Liz."

It was Friday morning, the House not sitting again until the following Tuesday.

"And the debate was adjourned." Order had not returned until late afternoon. "Probably helped save me from the Whip's vengeance. For once the crossbench not being ready was a blessing."

Like most major party politicians Order was irritated by the postponement of business because the small parties or independents were not prepared for the debate on legislation coming before the House. There was little sympathy for their heavier workload and lack of resources compared with their better staffed opponents: if you can't handle it don't field candidates was the general opinion and to Hell with democracy.

"April five gives us two weeks from tomorrow," Order continued, skipping the preliminaries because Liz knew what he was talking about. "Did Jayson get all the no junks among the preselectors?"

"Most." Liz unrolled a map of the electorate. "This area he couldn't cover in the time. Seventeen addresses."

"I'll check them over the weekend. You know yesterday's stuff-up has worked out better than I'd hoped. If Arnie's transport is available on Monday, we deliver early to the walkers an' then post to our people, say next Friday?"

"How *is* Mrs. Cohen?"

"Still in hospital, I suppose. We'll have to check."

Order was annotating the list of the fifty four preselectors who would decide his fate when Liz reported back upon the patient.

"They're keeping her in for a few days, John, just to make sure the head injury isn't serious."

"Send flowers."

"Already done."

Order had reason to be content upon this another glorious day when the changing colour of the leaves, especially those of the claret ash outside his window, were blindingly beautiful.

Mrs. Cohen safely tucked up in hospital and Rabbit's husband home for the weekend gave him time to concentrate upon the main issue.

"It's a very rough guesstimate," he told his secretary, "but I reckon I can count on twenty sure votes. I've put Bennett's at twelve. This leaves -"

"Twenty two," said Liz, who also could count.

"Eight more will do it."

"Not convincingly, John. You don't want to scrape in. The victory margin will leak out to the media an' you'll be seen as a lame duck candidate for the election."

You're right, Order silently agreed. I've got to wipe the floor with her.

"Lorraine Bennett might be behind at the moment," Liz continued remorselessly, "but she'll be doing her sums too. And she has your friend Prentice and possibly Davenport helping her."

"I'll have to see these people or most of them," he began.

"All of them, John," Liz interrupted and, seeing his expression, added: "Even your opponent's known supporters."

"A big job. I've only a fortnight an' the sitting week complicates matters. I can't just look in an' out, y'know. Best I can average I reckon is two a night."

"You will have to do your best. Remember, Lorraine Bennett's got the edge on you here. She's taken leave, I understand, and is sure to spend this fortnight visiting the preselectors."

While I'm stuck in the parliament, Order thought despondently, as Liz picked up his beeping telephone.

"Mr. Conrad," she said, handing him the receiver.

"How did you get on with Mrs. Cohen?" Abrupt again.

Order explained what had happened.

"She's in for a few days. Observation. I haven't spoken to her; she was unconscious when we took her to hospital."

"Where?"

Order told him.

"I trust she makes a full recovery."

"So do I. An' I'll ask her about the papers first chance I get," he promised.

"Thank you."

People always were hanging up on him.

"You're no worse off with Bennett out and about than you will be in an election," said Liz, resuming their conversation as if she had read his mind.

Which was true and a good reason for early preselection of candidates in opponent held seats. Nothing was more unnerving to a member holding a marginal constituency than the knowledge your challenger was out in the electorate getting themselves known, while you sat anchored in the parliament day after precious day.

"We'll have to plan this sensibly. How about I concentrate initially on the twenty two unknowns then move to my supporters an' lastly to theirs?"

"As good a strategy as any. You sure Bennett's twelve are definitely against you?"

"I think so. They're the hard core who voted for Bob before the by-election. Well, eleven anyway an' Judas Prentice."

"Jayson found fifteen no junk letterboxes an' you've another seventeen to check out."

"There'll be an overlap of my supporters an' hers," cautioned Order.

"But that needn't be a disadvantage if we post the newsletter to them all with a nice covering letter saying how we respect their wish for no unsolicited mail. You probably won't get more than five or six out of the seventeen addresses still to be checked, so we could easily personalise each letter."

"An' I top an' tail them with a handwritten salutation?"

"Can't do any harm. I'll start drafting the letter now, and then I can type them up and have them ready for say, next Friday?"

Nothing like an experienced staffer, Order told Rob Glasson and Tim Forbes over their regular Friday lunch in the parliamentary dining room.

"You can keep your dolly birds."

"No arguments from me," said Glasson, "but the young chicks have their uses."

"You're sounding like Brian."

"I didn't mean it that way," Glasson, who was loyally married, explained patiently. "They vote too, y'know."

Opposite him, Tim Forbes was looking uncomfortable. "Are you relying on the votes in here for the preselection?" he asked.

"Well, yes. I suppose so. I know you can't take anything or anyone for granted in this game but yes, I thought Rob's secretary an' Fearless Leader's front desk receptionist, Jim Terry an' Maureen from King's office …"

"I'm pretty sure my Sarah will stay with you," said Glasson, lowering his voice as a group of government backbenchers moved past deeper into the dining room. "Jim Terry too, 'though he hasn't any track record. He's only been in your electorate six month's or so, but he thinks you're okay."

His confident mood was gone. In spite of his earlier qualification Order *was* relying upon Party staffers support, indeed he'd factored them into his twenty sure votes.

"Maureen an' Avril?" he croaked, remembering the receptionist's name.

"I don't think so, John," said Forbes gently. "The sisterhood has been busy."

"My Carol heard it from Lorraine herself," Glasson confirmed. "You know they're in the Women's Institute together."

"Maybe that's the point. Bennett tells your wife, knowing it will get back to me? Psychological warfare."

"Can you risk it?"

You know I bloody well can't, thought Order. Eighteen, fourteen now. At least.

"How many more, I wonder?"

"Might be a good idea to check out the number of female preselectors and give them special attention, John," advised Forbes. "I'll get you another drink."

As his friend moved towards the bar, Glasson asked: "You haven't got Selby offside, have you, John?"

SIXTEEN

With no shopping centre duty on Saturday morning Order mopped up the seventeen outstanding addresses of his pre-selection list. As predicted there were only six more no junk mail letterboxes.

He did the checking without enthusiasm. The activities of the sisterhood had undermined his confidence and a call to Bernie on Friday afternoon had done nothing to lift his spirits.

The old Party secretary had been too wily to take sides.

"Everyone's entitled to stand, John, and the way the Government's going I think we've a chance next time, which only encourages more people to have a go."

"What are *my* chances?"

"Up to you. I'd expect you to be doorknocking the electorate again this weekend, but I wouldn't range too far. Just say, fifty four people?"

Now mid-afternoon Sunday he sat alone at an outdoor café gloomily assessing his situation. Weekends he usually welcomed as the chance to get out into the electorate to meet and greet friends, be seen by constituents and listen to their concerns. Very occasionally he would take in a film or drive out into the country.

The weekend had been overcast, the wind cool, and this weather seemed to affect Canberra's citizens. Nobody had wanted to stop and talk when he went shopping; the function on Saturday night had been boring and his hosts inattentive, as if they already had written him off as someone not worth cultivating.

Such depressing circumstances had carried over in his pre-selection visits. Saturday afternoon had coincided with televised warm-up football matches. Sunday morning was a visit no-no unless you were going to drinks and at two of the three homes he visited in the afternoon the Party members were out.

The reaction of the four, well seven people in all, he had spoken with over the weekend worried him. They were distant, reluctant to engage in conversation. With the exception of the Warburg's, who simply were irritated at his interruption of their AFL viewing, Order thought everyone else was positioning themselves as undeclared in the forthcoming contest. Wanting to be on the winning side, he decided bitterly.

It was several seconds before he realised the reverberation was not his heart but the locked off mobile phone in his breast pocket.

"Mr. Order? It's Gladys Bennett. Mrs. Cohen's friend."

"How is Mrs. Cohen, Mrs. Bennett?"

"She's coming home tomorrow. That's what I'm ringing about."

"She wants a lift?"

"No, not that. I think the ambulance will do that. No. I went to get her some clean clothes, you know I've got a key."

"Yes, Mrs. Bennett. I know," he said patiently.

"Well she's been broken into. Her house, I mean."

Mrs. Bennett was waiting for him at her front door.

"I didn't want to stay over there, Mr. Order. I was frightened."

"Of course. Let's have a look together," he said with more assurance than he felt.

The lounge room was as he remembered it and in answer to his unspoken question Mrs. Bennett led him through the house to the main bedroom.

"I came to get a dressing gown an' things," the old lady explained.

Order had expected a scene of chaos.

Usually, he'd been told, thieves trashed a property, sometimes worse. The sight was nothing as bad, nevertheless all drawers of the dressing table and the chest of drawers had been pulled out and closer inspection showed someone had riffled through the contents.

"Well," he began doubtfully.

"No, it's not like Lydia. She's a very tidy person. Besides, she's in hospital."

The kitchen was the same, drawers pulled out and the one containing papers thoroughly picked through.

They checked the other rooms but they revealed nothing. Mrs. Cohen obviously had closed off those parts of the house a widow living alone did not use. Only the telephone table drawer in the hallway had been similarly searched.

Any doubt he may have entertained about Mrs. Bennett's claim of her friend's tidiness was dispelled when he saw the flimsy lock on the back door inside an enclosed porch had been forced.

"We must get the police, Mr. Order."

"We don't know if anything's been stolen, Mrs. Bennett. Only Mrs. Cohen can tell us that."

Order didn't fancy another triple O call which might prove a waste of police time.

"You say Mrs. Cohen's coming home tomorrow? Why don't we leave everything as it is until then? We haven't touched anything an' she can decide what's been taken."

"We should call the police -" Mrs. Bennett's Neighbourhood Watch training asserted itself.

"There's nothing to go on. We don't know if anything's missing."

"They could take fingerprints. Search the area. Talk to the neighbours. You know, house to house canvass, isn't that what they do?"

In your television dreams, he thought.

"How about I phone my friend, Tim Forbes, an' ask his advice?

He's our police spokesman. We don't want to waste police time an' if he says we should, then we will. Otherwise, I'll drive you to the hospital with Mrs. Cohen's clothes."

"How did you get here before? Bus?" he asked Mrs. Bennett comfortable beside him in his nice car, as she described it, in a vain attempt to change the subject.

"Yes. I had to go through the interchange. Such a bother but I just have my pension so public transport's the only way. I hope your friend knows what he's talking about."

Forbes had been at a local football match but Order picked up from a noisy background of barracking that his own doubts had been correct.

"It's too tenuous, John. With nothing to go on they'd be wasting their time. It would probably be tomorrow anyway before they showed up. Thanks to this government's penny-pinching there's only two cars on duty right now covering each side of the lake."

Order had explained Forbes' advice, leaving out the thinness of the blue line so as not to worry Mrs. Bennett, and with some furniture they had secured the forced back door.

"I'm worried about telling Mrs. Cohen," continued his passenger. "We don't want to give her another heart attack."

"Let's leave it until tomorrow an' see how well she is," Order replied, confident he'd be nowhere near the old patient then.

Any conscience searching about keeping such worrying information from a sick old lady was eased by the nurse.

"She's asleep."

Depositing the clothes they quietly took their leave, but not before Order assured himself one of the two bouquets of flowers was his own.

Curious though.

For someone who was not involved with nor interested in Mrs. Cohen, Marek Conrad exhibited considerable concern about her well-being, as the second bouquet attested.

SEVENTEEN

"**G**abby?"

"No news, John. Their Sabbath an' then ours."

"No, I wanted to ask another favour."

It was a long shot, Order agreed with himself, after the policeman politely, firmly and tersely refused to seek details of Conrad's return flight from Melbourne with Qantas. Williams was equally unhelpful about the break-in.

"Happens all the time, John. Kids usually, especially in school holidays. What's the address?"

Order provided it, uncomfortable the incident *was* important and he should have reported it yesterday.

"I'll have a car drive past. Should frighten off any repeat," Williams concluded, hanging up.

The Monday Party room meeting had been a subdued affair. Preselection nominations closed at five o'clock that afternoon and Lorraine Bennett was not the only challenger to a sitting member. Bernie was giving nothing away but the rumour mill had firmed to three, possibly four, being under threat.

The question was who were they? Nobody could be sure and everyone in the room was nervous. For some this was because they thought they might be facing a preselection fight, while others confident of their position were looking further ahead and wondering if new and ultimately successful election candidates would alter the factional balance of power in the next parliament and thus advance or impede their own ambitions.

Collecting a nomination form, even collecting the requisite twenty signatures, in itself meant nothing. There always were a few non-starters: people who reassessed their chances, people who simply got cold feet, even the odd mischief maker who initially entered the lists for no other reason than to spook a sitting member.

Some stood for hopeless seats against entrenched government members, taking pride if they reduced the winning majority by a fraction. Usually these candidates came forward much later and were often promising younger people pressed into service for experience and, if they performed creditably, the run for a winnable seat in the future.

Nevertheless, there were dark horses.

Apart from Order, lovesick or lecherous - take your pick - Brian, was the only other member known to be being challenged.

"Buchan reckons it's Clare's boyfriend," proffered Rob Glasson, as they sat waiting for the meeting to begin.

"He's got no hope, whoever it is," opined Tim Forbes.

"Howso?"

"Brian *lives* for his electorate, is why."

"As you would, John, if you had Brian's wife an' their four kids."

"Unkind Rob, but true. He'd probably even make it as an independent."

Order recalled the conversation later in the morning when he and Liz were reviewing his preselection votes.

"It's early days, of course," he explained to his secretary, "but the weekend didn't profit me one vote an' now the margin's narrowed to four."

"You can't be sure of that, John. People don't want to commit themselves this far out." Then realising the negative inference of her comment, Liz added: "Probably don't want to be taken for granted."

Order had seized upon her first remarks.

"That's what worry's me. There was no enthusiasm an' the Warburg's were bloody anti." He'd counted them as probable supporters.

"You did interrupt their football viewing. They'll get over it."

"If I do go down, what d'you reckon my chances are as an independent?" he asked quietly, as if the walls had ears.

Liz was not a political creature. Just loyal, sensible and honest.

"John, you're all independents at heart. You just can't get elected without party support. It's the compromise you accept, the price of influencing decisions and getting *some* of your ideas or ideals up, no matter how distorted in a final form."

Order was surprised at his secretary's comments, firmly and forcefully delivered.

"No go then?"

"No go, John. Think it through. As an independent you could only achieve anything in the parliament if you held, or were part of, the balance of power. D'you really think the existing crossbenchers will survive the next election if our lot and the government have anything to do with it?"

"Then there are the practical problems of the campaign. Where will you get bodies to help with letterboxing or manning polling booths? You probably think you've got strong support? Every politician does because they keep meeting people who vote for them, but it's an illusion. If you could count up all these committed John Order voters, you'd be lucky to tot up a few hundred. They only seem more numerous because you're meeting them irregularly at different times and places."

"It's the Party candidate who's supported. If you walk away you're a political leper an' probably a social pariah too."

"You've been rehearsing this," Order said with a grin, encouraged by the commonsense.

"I thought it might come up. Don't lose your friends as well as your preselection. Anyway, it's not over yet. Who can we call on for help? Glasson? Forbes? How about staffers you worked with here before you were elevated?"

"Nobody close anymore. You know what the burn-out is like."

Staff didn't stay long in parliamentary offices. There were exceptions like Liz, but such people regarded their position as an interesting job, no more.

For the rest many were here for experience or contacts, useful in the wider world of employment. Others hoped for political preferment, as had happened to Order himself, but usually were too impatient to wait around for more than a short time.

"Glasson an' Forbes are doing what they can -" he said, knowing it wasn't enough.

"Then let's look at the uncommitted list again and plot a schedule of visits over the next fortnight."

"What about opponents?"

"They can be added," said Liz, "but we should rearrange the order. Put those you think will support you into the *final* week and *after* the newsletter's been delivered."

"Some publicity might help," suggested Order, encouraged by his staffer's positive attitude.

"Talk to Jim Terry. Have we got anything?"

"Not really. This preselection business has tied me down. Everything else is on hold." He glanced guiltily to his left, where a paper avalanche was threatening from his in-tray.

"I know. I've kept the electoral matters ticking over, but we're hardly running at speed. Ask Jim anyway, he might have something you can tell your adoring public."

"There's Mrs. Cohen." Tentatively however.

"There's *not* Mrs. Cohen. That's not public property. There *is* Mrs. Bennett."

"What, that I'm confident of winning? A presumptuous statement which would probably alienate the few supporters I've still got?"

"The other one. Phoned earlier. Wants you to ring her. I'll take these lists back to my office."

Order found Gladys Bennett at Mrs. Cohen's house.

"She's home, Mr. Order. They don't keep them longer than they have to these days. Mother's with new babies get tossed out within twenty four hours. Not like in my day."

"How *is* Mrs. Cohen?"

"She's asleep."

"How did she react to the break-in?" Why was Mrs. Bennett always testing his patience?

"She didn't. She seems alright, but she hasn't any idea what happened. The knock on the head must have given her a memory loss. I don't think it's too bad, mind you. It'll come back; otherwise she'd still be in hospital, wouldn't she?" The doubt was in the old nurse's voice.

"I'm sure she would be, Mrs. Bennett. Are you going to stay with her for a while?"

"I think I should. Until she wakes up, at least."

"Would you ring me when she does, Mrs. Bennett? I'd like to see her."

He waited most of the afternoon; time well spent clearing up the backlog of work.

Liz was an efficient culler and the recycling bin in her office directly received more correspondence than ever came to his personal attention. What continued to surprise him however was the unremitting deluge of government reports and publications, association newsletters and periodicals, charity requests and invitations - occasionally even a letter from a constituent seeking his help.

There was no way you could be removed from any of these address lists, because unlike shareholders who were given the option whether or not they received a company's annual report, politicians were never asked. There was a significant industry dedicated to planning, producing and posting all of this largely unwanted paper and too many jobs were at stake to have them threatened by offering choice to the captive addressees.

Order had applied a yellow post-it label for direction to the office Crazies file to another of the Emperor of Papua-New Guinea's infrequent letters - easily recognised by the *Be It Know That* in well-crafted gothic script - when Mrs. Bennett telephoned.

"How is Mrs. Cohen?"

"She'd like to see you, Mr. Order," was the non-committal reply.

Mrs. Cohen was sitting in her dressing gown in a lounge room chair, a prominent plaster across the side of her forehead.

"Here's Mr. Order to see you, Lydia," said Mrs. Bennett, ushering him forward. "D'you mind if I slip home for a moment? I want to see if the washing's dry."

After a few perfunctory questions and answers about her state of health, Order began to fulfil his promise to the jewellery store magnate.

"Marek Conrad has spoken to me about your telephone conversation, Mrs. Cohen. He was upset about it an' is convinced you've got the wrong Korzeniowski."

Mrs. Cohen nodded at the Polish name but said nothing. A pleasant half-smile encouraged him to continue.

"He wants to help you find this fellow so the mix-up can be sorted out an' he said you mentioned some papers you had?"

Mrs. Cohen nodded agreeably again.

"Papers Daniel Levy might have given to you?"

"There's a Paul Levy I see at the Centre," Mrs. Cohen confirmed. "What does he want with me 'though?"

"No, Daniel Levy, Mrs. Cohen. The young man who visited you recently? From Israel?"

"I don't know what you're talking about, Mr. Order."

EIGHTEEN

"The knock on the head obviously has caused some memory loss," he told Liz as he noted down the names of the two pre-selection couples he was visiting that evening.

"Mrs. Bennett reckons it's only temporary an' it seems to be limited to the last couple of weeks because she recognised me."

"You sure?"

"Well, she thanked me for coming to see her."

"Probably being polite. Doesn't mean she knows who you are."

Which complicated matters, as a clearly unhappy Marek Conrad made plain during their brief telephone conversation.

"Keep in touch with her, Mr. Order, and report back to me as soon as you have something definite. I'm not having my name and reputation damaged by unfounded accusations."

"Can she take care of herself?" Liz continued.

"So Mrs. Bennett says. She's promised to keep an eye on her, but she reckons she's not physically or mentally knocked around, just this lapse about those events."

As he was about to leave for a meal, Bernie phoned.

"It's not looking too good," Order replied. "About eighteen fourteen, but I could've lost some of the unknowns by now."

If Order was hoping for something profound and uplifting from Bernie he didn't get it.

"Just keep working on the numbers, John, and remember, you're the sitting member." He paused. "Marek Conrad's phoned. You recall we spoke about them? The jewellers? He's not happy with you, John. I don't know why and I don't want to know, but just make sure you keep him onside. To cross someone like that will do more than lose you the preselection; it could seriously affect the Party itself. Am I making myself clear?"

No politician was told where election funds came from. Bernie worked strictly on a need-to-know basis only and although parliamentary members wondered if the Party sometimes sold its favours too cheaply as a result, there was nothing they could do about it.

"Loud an' clear, Bernie." Bloody chequebook politics.

"Keep working on your numbers, John."

Order thought about phoning Rabbit. The usual arrangement was she contacted him, upon the specious reasoning he was the busiest. An excuse they both knew was a lie: Order was practicing simple political caution and he followed it now.

"How did you go?" Liz asked next morning as he examined his draft programme for the Party meeting.

"The Earnshaws were out but the Bradley's were supportive. Back to twenty, I think."

"D'you think you should phone ahead?"

"I've decided we should after last night," he confirmed. "Only problem is Bennett's supporters. They'll make an excuse not to see me."

"Then we cold canvass them and set up appointments with the others."

With the closing of preselection nominations the Party room meeting was back to its usual turbulence, the attendees relaxed in most cases and resuming their eternal quest for political recognition and advancement.

Apart from Brian and himself there were two other sitting members facing challenges and nobody was predicting an upset with either of them.

Glasson and Forbes avoided the topic altogether during and

after the Party meeting, which closed with an appeal from Fearless Leader to pass on any leaks about the forthcoming Budget to the shadow treasurer's office.

The mention of Tony King brought home to Order his parlous level of preselection support among his own colleagues' staff and it didn't get any better upon his return to the office.

"The Wrights are going to be away," said Liz, who had been organising the evening's visits. "How did you fancy your support with them?"

"Only fifty-fifty. I don't know them very well. They've only been here from Adelaide a few months."

Anyway Lorraine can't get them either, he thought, and it reduces the majority needed.

"Jim Terry wants to know have you anything to say to the media? They're asking for comment."

"So they've finally got onto it." And reached the same conclusion as his colleagues that his preselection fight was the only game in town.

"What's Mother Hubbard think?" he asked the media officer.

Mother Hubbard was the nickname of the Opposition's Media Relations Section, or MRS for short, set up after several major public statements had been released simultaneously, thus diluting their electoral effect. Its job was to co-ordinate announcements and while viewed with suspicion by some backbenchers who believed it gave shadow ministers more exposure than they deserved and exercised undue censorship upon everyone else, its approval was mandatory for any media release or comment.

"No problem in principle. They want to see what you're planning to say, of course. Mustn't be contentious, as usual." Terry had his own difficulties with the old bitch.

"I'll prepare something bland but statesmanlike."

"I'll be in the House soon."

"No problem. It'll be lunch by the time I get it approved."

With the postponed education debate listed as the third item upon the day's programme, Order asked Liz to find out the condition of Mrs. Cohen's memory and hurried downstairs.

It didn't pay to leave your arrival late to participate in a debate. For many reasons the listed Order of Business could alter instantly. So Order always arrived in good time. He'd seen enough members stumbling through a speech, repeating themselves through lack of preparation, unsuccessfully trying to think upon their feet even as they spoke and ignorant of what had been said by previous participants.

There was a downside to this thoughtful anticipation: sitting through the earlier matter under debate, which usually held no interest. Worse, there was no time limit for its resolution.

Of the three great lies of the world, Order had added a fourth, albeit of more limited application, of a politician's assurance to the House: "I will be brief… "

These contributors were aided and abetted by their staff, who in part justified their existence by writing long speeches which ignored the Standing Order's speaking time limits. They did so knowing they would be supported by their member and a tolerant House would grant an extension of time. The former because whatever was said and no matter how longwinded was worth listening to - just ask them - and the latter because other members would seek the same indulgence when it was their turn to address their peers.

Conforming to the accepted wisdom the average member had a real attention span in a debate of the length of their own contribution, Order waited and wasted the morning session in the Chamber flicking through glossy government publications looking at pictures, as required by political correctness and multiculturalism, of people of various names and colours doing things together in social settings. He recognised nobody.

"Where's my media statement?" he called through to Liz upon his return to the office.

"Ring Jim Terry," his secretary said in a non-committal voice.

"Knocked on the head, John." The media man sounded embarrassed.

An idea of Bernie's, Terry was paid by the pooling of backbench members' excess staff salary allocations which individually did not stretch to employing another full-time office worker. He was fiercely loyal to his employers.

"Why? It's just a simple statement, you said."

"And it is, believe me."

"I'll phone Mother Hubbard myself. This is ridiculous."

"Not Mother Hubbard's decision, John. Leader's office." Terry *was* embarrassed.

"Selby?" Order guessed.

"Yep. Said the parliamentary wing shouldn't be seen to be taking sides."

"Mrs. Cohen?" Order barked to Liz, fighting to control his anger.

"Mrs. Bennett said Mrs. Cohen's mental condition is unchanged."

And still there was no message from Rabbit.

Order went out and bought a sandwich for lunch. Ostensibly he wanted fresh air but the reality was he didn't fancy making conversation in the dining room, even with Glasson and Forbes.

Politics was a lonely occupation. Many acquaintances but few friends, as Bernie had explained. And it was uncanny how quickly people picked up the whiff of a dying career, or so it seemed to Order, because he met nobody upon his brief walk, no cheerful hellos nor friendly waves, not even The Battler, a local character who importuned for spare change.

The afternoon brought no relief from his gloom.

Liz, he decided, was avoiding him. He had no question to ask when the House met for the daily verbal punch-up and afterwards the morning's debate dragged on interminably as chance not tactical planning created a talk fest.

There was a stage with some legislation when members

unilaterally decided they must speak, a lemming-like urge which drew them into the Chamber as surely as to the cliff over which the doomed rodents allegedly plunged.

It was tame and boring. There is a limit to what a series of speakers can say upon any particular matter, especially as talk-back radio callers and letters-to-the-editor writers have more real freedom of expression than any politician.

The division bells were stridently demanding everyone's presence for the vote, members prolonging the call to its maximum time by ambling in, when Jack, the attendant, handed him the message.

I sit here all afternoon doing nothing then I'm called when I'm required for a division and my matter's coming on. Not my day, Order decided, scribbling a note he would telephone Marek Conrad as soon as he could, calling Jack through the attendants' button to pass the message back to Liz.

Voluntary school fees encouraged another marathon debate, with member after member rising to contribute very little new to what already had been said. The problem was, Order guessed, most members had personal experience of voluntary fees and therefore could claim expertise in the subject.

Another caprice of long debates then asserted itself: amendments.

What should have been a simple choice for the parliament to vote to make the fees mandatory instead of voluntary was complicated by a crossbench move to limit the compulsory nature of the alternative proposal to those who could afford to pay. This amendment was further and successfully changed after tiresome argument to allow individual schools to make this financial judgment. The suggestion proved too much for a minor Party, who then moved the matter go back to the education committee for reconsideration.

Julie Davenport, still smarting over her rebuke from Eric White for not originally dissenting and a few more recent jibes from the government benches for her change of mind at this late stage, sought to have the Opposition support the referral back to the committee.

Telling Order to be prepared to speak again if necessary and defend the Party's position, White took Julie Davenport into the lobby to remind her of the agreed policy and, Order hoped, beat her to death.

Eventually all amendments were put and lost by a series of unholy alliances whereby strange party groupings formed together to defeat others and the Government's original proposal was passed.

It was late when Order telephoned back to the jeweller, very tired after almost an entire and largely wasted day in the Chamber.

"I'm not used to being kept waiting, Order," Conrad stated in his all too usual authoritative tone.

"Sorry. I've been tied up in the House."

"To Hell with the House. When I want to speak with you, you speak! Understood?"

"Go screw yourself, Conrad." And John Order hung up.

NINETEEN

Order had no opportunity to ruminate upon his temper tantrum on the cool Wednesday morning. Liz too had seen the newspaper.

"Lorraine Bennett doesn't have the constraints of the parliamentary party's even- handedness, John," she explained unnecessarily.

Yet, he thought, glaring at the photograph and the diplomatic comment about her chances in the preselection ballot beneath a sub-editor's headline *Out of Order?*

"How many will see it anyway, John, far less read the story? You know you have to feature on pages one, three or the back page to get any real attention."

This was kind but not true, because several of his colleagues in commiserating terms commented to him about the news item before the Party meeting began.

The Whip had him down for Chamber duty again for the first hour of the morning session, although Order could not recall how he had offended, unless Conrad's influence stretched into parliamentary rosters. Anyway, it kept him out of the office and away from telephone calls. Liz could monitor Mrs. Cohen's condition.

He was surprised when he returned from duty to find there were no messages. No Conrad, no Rabbit and, more importantly, no Bernie.

"Don't forget you've a committee meeting at twelve-thirty, then the gumboot throwing competition at five-thirty, if you rise in time," said Liz. "I'll organise another two preselector visits for tonight."

"Cancel the gumboots. I'm not in the mood. An' where's Jayson? He's here Wednesday isn't he?"

"You sure about the gumboots? It's for charity."

"Positive. Anyway, if we sit beyond five-thirty it'll be too dark." He paused. Might as well be honest. "I'm not keen to do it, Liz. I'm becoming cautious about silly stunts."

Like the great no junk mail debate, there were two equally strong opinions about participating in oddball fundraising activities. One school claimed your involvement was good publicity and showed you as a caring person, while the contra school argued you looked foolish and most of the electorate thought you were doing it for selfish political reasons. The organisers cared nothing for such nuances, they only wanted public figures.

"Jayson?" he prompted.

"He's not coming in today."

"Why not?"

"I don't know, John. His excuse wasn't very convincing."

"Liz, are we losing this?"

"Again, I don't know."

"Bloody fair-weather friends," he said angrily.

"The stress is showing in your language, so be careful. And if we *are* losing, let's go down fighting."

Adopting an aggressive do or die attitude in the privacy of your office didn't translate easily into wider society.

"I see you've a fight on your hands," said feisty Wendy Wonder, Volkswagen, herself unchallenged - nobody would dare, Order believed - when she joined him at the committee meeting.

"I'll make it," he muttered unconvincingly as the Chairman, Jim Rhodes, called the members to order.

They were conducting pre-Budget discussions with community groups and at the best of times Order found the exercise trying.

The witnesses coming before them each held the unshakeable

conviction their particular organisation, irrespective of the economic climate, should be singled out for favourable consideration.

They each claimed, supported by submissions running to pages of paper, they were on the verge of bankruptcy. Nothing less than a substantial injection of taxpayers' money could save from collapse the essential work they were doing. Work, they were quick to point out which would cost the government considerably more money if the public purse took over the operation.

Always assuming any government would bother to do so, Order often asked himself.

The committee members were sympathetic, patient and gave nothing away. They knew from experience these hearings rarely revealed much more than the prejudices of the witnesses for their own area of interest.

Except Wendy Wonder.

Volkswagen was ambitious. Reputedly after Harold Chambers' job of Opposition Whip, a quest which was the regular subject of dirty gossip, she also held to a strong belief she and her colleagues would be occupying the Treasury benches following the next election.

This unbridled optimism made VW politically foolhardy and a continuing irritation to Jim Rhodes as he tried to rein in her extravagant guarantees to the many money hungry groups coming before them. For his part Order silently sided with the Government chairman, worried the wild promises in opposition would be the broken promises in government.

"The committee is not here to give any undertaking. We have no mandate to do so," Rhodes said often, in exasperation. Nevertheless, Wendy Wonder persevered.

The last group's hearing concluded, Chairman Rhodes brought the meeting to an end and the committee members and the witnesses gathered their papers and prepared to leave the room.

As they moved there was an inevitable contact between the two groups. Order was proceeding to the door when he was intercepted.

"Paul Reynolds, Mr. Order. From the Jewish Centre - though I'm not here on their behalf. We spoke on the phone."

A thickset man, balding, untidy, with a greying beard. They shook hands.

"How's Mrs. Cohen? Sort everything out?"

Order explained what had happened.

"I'm sorry. I didn't know. We'll send someone from our welfare volunteers to see her."

"I'm sure that would be appreciated. Mrs. Cohen has a temporary memory loss, as I understand. Seeing someone she knows from the Centre might help her recovery."

"Not much chance of that," said Reynolds, with a quick glance to his departing community colleagues. "Mrs. Cohen attends our religious observances but nothing else."

"You knew her well enough to direct that boy," he paused, "Levy to her."

"Oh yes. He had information. Only needed an address."

He was moving; conscious his fellow witnesses were leaving the room and would want to conduct an assessment outside of their performance before the committee.

Order had an urgent inspiration.

"Information, Paul? Written information? Papers perhaps?"

Reynolds still was moving and Order accompanied him, friendly like.

"Nice to have met you, Mr. Order," the man said at the door of the committee room. "Yes, Levy did say he had some papers to show Mrs. Cohen. Now, if you'll excuse me I must catch my friends…"

TWENTY

Again with no question to ask and no role in the afternoon session's agenda, Order before returning to his office as required dutifully sat through the daily slaughter known as Question Time.

And it was a slaughter.

All governments are infallible. Only ex-governments - the opposition - have made mistakes, the twisted logic being that that is why they are ex-governments.

Everyone in the Chamber knew their chances of media coverage from a question or an answer was remote. A few wits tried to be quoted by pithy quick comments, which the majority of the politicians believed would be lost upon the journalists who covered the sittings and reported on only from spoon-fed media releases. Investigative political journalism was dead in this city.

Therefore the battle was conducted within the Chamber exclusively for the participants.

The badly constructed question which allowed a simple yes or no answer, the slip in a reply which caused the Opposition hounds to try to run down their Government quarry with a supplementary question. Even the occasional breach of Standing Orders allowing Speaker Harris to rule a question out-of-order because it asked for an opinion or sought a yet-to-be announced policy decision.

The Opposition occasionally could score a psychological point.

Bob Buchan was adept at this verbal warfare.

"Mr. Speaker, I had hoped to ask a question of the Minister for Transport, but he's not here. Hardly surprising, given the mess this Government -"

"Ask your question," ordered Speaker Harris, as the Minister scurried back to his seat from consulting departmental officers sitting behind the government benches.

Or later, Buchan again.

"Mr. Speaker. Point of order. Surely it's enough that we have to listen to a Dorothy Dix question from the Government backbench without the member who asked it walking out without listening to the reply?"

"The Chair cannot compel a member to listen to anything. There is no point of order - as you well know," said Speaker Harris resignedly.

"Who have we got for tonight?" Order asked back in his office.

"Mr. Hammond and the Graces. You'll have to make an early call on Mr. Hammond; he goes to bed at eight o'clock he tells me."

"So he can walk his dogs at six a.m." Order confirmed, remembering the doggy smell which pervaded the widower's home from his only other visit.

"No calls?" he ventured.

"None."

"Not even Mrs. Cohen?"

"Mrs. Bennett will phone if there's a change. Otherwise I'll contact her each day."

Order spent the afternoon signing off the no junk letters and attending to incoming mail. The House rose early enough for him to visit Mr. Hammond and his doggy smell house then on to the Graces.

"Difficult to say, Liz," he reported Thursday morning. "They were all very non-committal. I'm not even sure Ted Hammond knew what I was talking about. His concentration is worsening."

Again he had no role in the proceedings of the parliament and was beginning to think this was deliberate. No action so no possibility of even chance publicity.

"Mrs. Cohen's still the same and the Hardy's said not to bother calling on them because you've got their vote," said Liz when he returned from the fruitless Party meeting.

"Best news I've heard. Gives me what? Twenty two?"

"Right on the button. With sixteen now unknown - at least to us."

"Probably closer though. Bennett will have picked up a few, I suppose."

Order was despondent. Nothing appeared to be working for him. He was in a political black hole and even other matters in his life were going nowhere.

No word from Rabbit, no rebuke from Bernie for his treatment of the influential jeweller, no change to Mrs. Cohen's condition.

Gabby Williams completed the negatives.

"I'll let you know as soon as Israel tells us, John," he said testily, hanging up.

"Mrs. Green said you can meet her at the club at lunchtime if you want to talk to her. She won't open her door at night to anyone," Liz called through. "You've a community meeting tonight anyway. Buy her lunch," she added. "Today?"

"Okay."

Mrs. Green's concern for her safety at night probably was genuine, however Order later decided the badge draw and the meat tray raffle at the club also influenced her thinking. And despite her protests she ate almost nothing these days she took little urging to tuck into the roast lamb and veg special.

He came away reasonably confident he had Madge - call me Madge, please - Green's vote, although it was difficult to be sure with the conversation stopper of the club employee's intrusive call of the winning meat tray numbers.

"Well, as you know Mrs. - Madge - I've only been a member -"

"Two three seven. Who's got lucky two three seven?"

"Pardon?"

"I've only been a member for less than -"

"Two three seven. Final call. Ah, here we are. Bit slow off the mark, aren't you?"

Everybody with a microphone loves the power it gives them, thought Order, trying again.

"An' I'd like the chance to continue to -"

"Next tray an' we have twenty one. Who's got twenty one?"

"I'm not doing well today, Mr. Order," said Madge Green, fanning her tickets out on the tablecloth, unwittingly echoing his own thoughts.

Thursday must be badge draw day throughout Canberra, Order decided that night, sitting in a sparsely attended meeting of a local suburban pressure group, while yet another mike maniac next door drowned out the chairman's reading of the minutes.

As if it mattered.

His experience of public meetings was they often were chaired by verbose people.

Order was not here to seek preselection votes; none of the Party faithful were present. Rather, taking advantage of the parliament rising early for a two week break, he was attending to learn more details of a proposal to upgrade a local oval, an issue which had become contentious because a stand of trees was to be removed to accommodate a building to house public toilets and a canteen.

Inevitably, being Canberra, there was support from the sporting fraternity and the local school and opposition from environmentalists.

Two departmental officers sat quietly in the front row of seats, waiting their turn to outline the brief.

It was a good half hour before they were called and Order sensed rather than saw the room filling up around and behind him. He had adopted his usual tactic of burying himself in the middle of a meeting when he was present only as a listener.

When the chairman finally gave up the limelight the departmental officials rose and delivered a bland, largely irrelevant publicity promo about the development, repeatedly stressing no decision yet had been reached by the government. They also handled out a coloured photocopied sheet of the site, in case somebody had wandered in off the street unfamiliar with the issue. The badge draw broadcast had concluded.

"Thank you for that detailed explanation," the chairman began.

"Questions," called someone to the back of the room.

"Our guests can't stay long," said the chairman. "It was good enough of them to come along an' give up their own time -"

"We have a right to questions, chairperson," called a strident female voice.

Grudgingly the chair allowed the opportunity and the environmental opponents began their assault.

It was a one-sided exchange because as the departmental representatives repeatedly stated they had no authority to give any undertakings. That was the government's prerogative. Or no, they couldn't comment upon that aspect either because it was the responsibility of another department.

"What's the point of coming here then?" growled a bearded obviously angry young man.

Others in the audience thought this was unfair and a verbal skirmish had to be silenced by the chair.

Order marvelled at the dexterity of the public servants in avoiding any commitment. They reminded him of experienced tail-end batsmen playing out time.

He'd seen similar performances before - which did not detract from his admiration each time they occurred - just as he'd seen the same paradox from members of the public, normally so critical of government expenditure but now calling for profligate amounts of taxpayers dollars to be spent to satisfy their pet concern, the trees.

He sensed the meeting was winding down. The stonewalling by the bureaucrats had convinced all but the most persistent of questioners that there was no further information to be gained. The night was cold and the audience was thinking of the comfort of their homes or a drink at the club's bar.

"What do our politicians think about the proposal?" said a familiar voice behind him.

"They're not here - as usual," came an equally usual interjection.

"John Order is," said the voice. "What does he think?"

"I didn't see you, Mr. Order," apologised the chair.

And I didn't identify myself because I didn't want to be acknowledged and so drawn into this divisive issue, Order silently admitted, rising to his feet and turning to address his unhelpful constituent.

Wearing jeans, a sweater beneath an anorak and a hard smile, Lorraine Bennett awaited his comments.

TWENTY ONE

"I took a leaf out of the bureaucrats' book, Liz," he recounted the next morning.

"And?"

"Told the multitude until there was a firm proposal from government we would not make a decision. Idle to speculate. Seemed to be well received."

"She's after you."

I'm getting used to it, he decided, and wondered if Lorraine Bennett was getting nervous. "Did Arnie deliver the newsletter to the walkers yesterday?"

Order usually helped move the several thousand sheets but he'd been Housebound.

"No problems and he wished you luck."

"He'll send in his account, I hope? Okay, then let's get these no junks enveloped, stamped and dispatched."

"Mrs. Cohen?" he asked, as they rubber banded the bundles for posting.

"I've still to ring Mrs. Bennett."

And what if this condition is permanent worried Order. Where were the papers Reynolds had confirmed existed? If Conrad had them already, why was he so keen to have Order talk to the old lady? Was the jeweller's interest more than a need to clear up a case of mistaken identity?

This limbo with other people with whom he was involved was equally worrying.

Rabbit had been incommunicado all week and now her husband would be home for the weekend. How long did it take for the results of a pregnancy test anyway?

Bernie too had been off the air. Granted, he didn't make a habit of phoning members when the parliament was sitting, but Order had expected some reaction from the Party machine after his exchange with the jeweller if the man was as influential as Bernie claimed.

Then there was Conrad himself. He didn't strike Order as the sort of person who would forget an issue or for that matter, an insult.

"How many do I still have to visit?" he asked Liz when she reported back there was no change to Mrs. Cohen's condition.

"With a week to go, too many. At least six undecided, well three because they're couples, then there are about ten hopefully your supporters and fourteen known in Bennett's camp."

"I can't do it, Liz. Tonight and Saturday night's out, say two tomorrow afternoon, Sunday afternoon another what, three? Then next week."

"Only to Thursday, John. You'll look desperate trying Friday, the day before preselection. And you need time to prepare your speech."

The shift to two income families did not help: only the retired could be visited during the working week.

"Priority to the undecided, then my known supporters an' Bennett's only if there's time."

"Or opportunity. If you're in the neighbourhood say. Also, Sunday might be out. You've got a doorknock."

Order remembered Bernie's advice last year, after he had missed the seasonal collections.

"Do a charity doorknock, John. Just to be seen to be helping *without* fanfare."

The Salvo's, St Vincent de Paul, Red Cross, to name a few. There were plenty to choose from and he had accepted the Party secretary's wise suggestion.

"It'll take your mind off the preselection," Liz said gently, reading his irritated reaction.

"I could still do both."

"Of course. Depends where you're assigned. If you're climbing steep driveways, perhaps only to find people aren't home, you mightn't feel enthusiastic to do preselection house calls in the afternoon."

Charity doorknocks were the only acceptable intrusion upon a resident's Sunday morning privacy.

According to Tim Forbes many people did not respond to your visit. Away at the coast, sleeping off a Saturday night hangover, making love. Some even at church.

Those who did answer their door were, depending upon the respect held for the particular charity, as generous as their circumstances allowed, averred Forbes, although some who had expensive houses gave very little, charity beginning and ending at home.

"I'll talk to Tim over lunch," Order decided.

"Doubt you can do both, John," his friend opined, as they sat in the deserted parliamentary dining room. "You'll find two hours on your feet very tiring, what with waiting for the door to be answered, then waiting while some money is found, then counting what is often spare change. And be careful. You're responsible for any shortfall between what's written on the receipt an' what's in the cash envelope."

"Thanks. It's useful advice to conserve myself if I'm calling on preselectors later."

"Don't fancy your chances all the same. You will be tired an' if it's warm probably sweaty too, which is no way to impress the punters. By the way, did you know the Kerrigan's are back?"

"They're overseas."

"They were. Back early. Ran out of money most likely. He's a terrible skinflint."

"How d'you know?"

"Kerrigan being tight-fisted? Oh, I see. No, we were looking after their bloody dog. No way would they pay kennel fees. Worth a visit, John. I don't know if they'd support you, but I'll bet the Bennett's don't know they're home."

Order knew he could put them in his supporter's group for a phase two visit. Back to fifty four with twenty four support?

Forbes proved to be correct. Order was footsore after two hours on Sunday collecting for charity.

Saturday afternoon's two visits had proved inconclusive, the Fergusons and the Swifts non-committal about their support, with Hetty Swift not sure she even would be at the preselection because her daughter was due to give birth any day in Albury.

The doorknock area he had been assigned was not mountainous. A pleasant middle class section of a suburb with an egalitarian mix of guvvie and private houses. The leaves were falling steadily now as autumn advanced and it was easy to identify the property proud from the tidy and untidy public footpaths in front of the houses.

He noted the developer's unoriginal designs for their relentless acquisition of old homes, slavishly copying each other's styles. You could chart the trendy architecture: Palladian, Doric, Federation, blockhouse, year after year.

Vodka and coke was holding up well among the young as was bottled water with the health freaks he also noted, seeing the discarded cans and plastic containers in the gutters and upon the nature strips.

Occasionally he saw the once scarred hills, where young but thickening gum and pine trees gradually were softening the devastation of the bushfire of the early millennium.

Tired but virtuous, he gladly accepted the offer of a cool drink from his friends and supporters, the Hardy's, when almost at the end of his tour he called in to thank them for their votes.

"You were lucky to find us home, John," said Mrs. Hardy as she handed him the glass of lemonade. "We're expecting our grand-children, so we didn't go."

Bert Hardy's warning look was too late.

"Go where?"

"Oh I'm sorry, John," Muriel Hardy was flustered. "But you'll find out anyway."

"Find out what?" asked Order, suddenly alert.

"My wife was referring to Lorraine Bennett's Sunday brunch today for all pre-selectors," Bert said bluntly. "Not that it would have changed our vote, mind."

"Thank you. You'd be more comfortable here anyway, fifty odd people is a lot to squeeze into a town house."

"Oh it wasn't at the Bennett's, John. It was at that man Conrad's, the jeweller."

TWENTY TWO

Order finished his doorknock, paid in his collection, including the two dollar shortfall, and dejectedly began his drive home.

If it hadn't been for the hands free facility he would not have bothered to answer the mobile.

"It's Mrs. Bennett, Mr. Order."

"Hello, Mrs. Bennett," he said wearily. "How's Mrs. Cohen?"

"No change when I last saw her, Mr. Order. I don't see her all the time now because the Jewish people have sent a woman to visit. It's such a relief to have the watch shared. Not that I mind, you know, because Lydia's no trouble, no trouble at all. She just can't remember."

"We must be patient, Mrs. Bennett," Order said without believing it.

"Of course. But that's not why I phoned you."

"No?" He was going to have an accident; his own patience was so strained.

"No. A man called to see Lydia. I wasn't there and neither was the Jewish woman. He had a lovely black car. Better than yours, Mr. Order, if you'll pardon me."

"Can you describe him?" Order knew he was wasting his breath.

"Well, I only saw him from my window. Thickset and, yes, bald. Didn't stay long."

"And?"

"Well I thought I should check on Lydia, but she didn't know who he was or what he was talking about. She said he asked about some papers."

"Huh, huh."

"Yes. And I wondered if they might be in the envelope I found underneath Lydia when we found her. I put it in my bag when she went to hospital and completely forgot about it. I still have it with me and it's addressed to you, Mr. Order."

"Mrs. Bennett, I'm on my way."

It was an old A4, doubled over and secured with a rubber band. Mrs. Cohen had written his name over her own in black marker.

"Are you going to open it, Mr. Order?"

He was perched upon the edge of a deep frayed lounge chair in Mrs. Bennett's front room.

"It's addressed to you," the old lady encouraged.

Inside was another middling size brown envelope with a cord wound around a button keeping it firmly closed. It was mottled, stained and smelled old.

Carefully he unwound the cord and shook out the contents into his right hand.

There were two pieces of paper. One was an official looking document, the other a typewritten letter. Both were faded and incomprehensible.

"That's not English," said Mrs. Bennett, who was peering inquisitively over his shoulder. "What is it?"

"I've no idea, but I'd guess the language is Polish."

"Then we'd better go and see Lydia. I was going over there anyway."

Mrs. Cohen, sitting in her chair beside the table with her tablets within easy reach, greeted them warmly.

"It really is good of you to visit me so regularly, Mr. Order. I'm sure you're a very busy man. You don't have to you know. Gladys and my friends at the Centre take good care of me."

"I'm sure they do, Mrs. Cohen, but I have a reason to see you today. You addressed this envelope to me."

Order had returned the package to the larger envelope, to the way he'd received it.

"Really?" Mrs. Cohen's expression retained the incomprehension her two friends had come to know so well.

"Yes. An' I wondered, well, if you still wanted me to have it?" Order handed her the envelope.

Slowly, carefully, she removed the rubber band, took out the second envelope, unwound the cord and shook out the papers.

Mildly curious was the way Order described her behaviour as watched by him and Mrs. Bennett she glanced through the two pages.

"Ah yes. These are the documents Daniel Levy left with me," she said, nodding to herself.

"Mrs. Cohen!" they exclaimed simultaneously.

"You're better!" added Gladys Bennett.

"How did you get hold of these?" Mrs. Cohen looked worried. "I meant to give them to you, but I don't believe that I did."

"A long story -" began Order.

"You've not been well," interrupted Mrs. Bennett and together they filled in the missing days of Lydia Cohen's life.

They listened out in embarrassed silence her thanks for their help and finally accepted her assurance she now had recovered.

"Then I'll be off, Mrs. Cohen. I've had a long tiring day 'though your recovery has seen it end on a happier note."

"I'd put those papers away somewhere safe," he added, remembering the break-in and Conrad's visit, which neither he nor Gladys Bennett had mentioned. "They might be important."

"That's what I think too, but I'm not sure yet." Mrs. Cohen handed the packet back to him. "I want you to keep them in a safe place for me. Can you do that?"

"Of course." Order didn't have a security box and a locked desk drawer in his office would not suffice. Harold Chambers probably would oblige, but if the Whip was out of sorts with him again there was always his bank.

"There's something else I'd like you to do for me, Mr. Order." the old lady continued. "Could you get me copies of those papers? Photocopies? You have such machines in your parliament?"

"In my own office, Mrs. Cohen."

"Do the best you can. They're very old and faded, I appreciate. You've probably guessed what I intend to do?" The old eyes twinkled. "Yes, the language is Polish and I want to translate them into English, or as much as my rusty memory will allow me to do."

"When would you like them? Today?"

"Tomorrow will be time enough," she said with what Order thought was a tone of resignation. "It will take me a few more days anyway. I might even have to get to a library. I suppose they have dictionaries?"

Promising to deliver the copies on Monday, Order took his leave accompanied by an excited Mrs. Bennett.

"What do you think they're about, Mr. Order?" She grasped his arm as they waded through the fallen leaves.

"I've no idea," he replied, only half lying, "but I think it would be very sensible to keep what we've seen an' heard a secret between the three of us."

"Don't worry about me, Mr. Order. My memory's like a sieve. Took me over a week to give you the envelope, remember?"

TWENTY THREE

The Monday Party meeting was a scrappy affair. Members raising various issues which had been postponed for discussion because of the more immediate matters of sitting weeks.

Order didn't pay much attention, preoccupied with assessing his chances for next Saturday after Conrad's generous hosting of Sunday drinks for his challenger. The political grapevine had picked it up, of course, and he received a number of back slaps and arm grips from colleagues wishing him luck.

Glasson and Forbes did their best to put as good a spin as possible upon his situation, but they were not convincing. Everyone who took an interest now realised the fight on his hands was of Waterloo proportions.

It provided him with a brief respite to obtain the clearest photocopies for Mrs. Cohen and he diligently worked the machine's buttons lightening and darkening the copies until he was satisfied he'd done the best possible job. As an extra precaution he fed the spoiled papers into the shredder down the corridor.

"I'll take these to Mrs. Cohen, Liz. Then I'll see the Kerrigan's. They're back an' I don't think Bennett knows, so I'll need to strike quickly before Conrad puts on a private dinner party for them."

"Stay focussed and confident, John," Liz said loyally, although Order wondered if she really believed herself in his victory chances. "Not everybody's going to be impressed enough to change their vote by a luxury house and cheap champagne."

Only a majority, thought Order, an' who said the bubbly was cheap?

"Don't turn down any good job offers, Liz, *if* they're offered," he said seriously, aware of the difficulties staffers of defeated members had finding other employment.

"Piss off," she said uncharacteristically, but smiling.

Mrs. Cohen received him at her door and in the lounge room inspected the photocopies and told him with thanks they were clear enough to translate.

"I'll phone you when I've finished, Mr. Order," she said dismissively but smiling. "I owe you that much."

Mrs. Bennett waved to him from her front window as he walked toward his car, crunching down what seemed to be even more leaves.

The Kerrigan's were inner city residents, a short distance from Mrs. Cohen's home allowing for road works. These repairs constantly were underway and often had been used by Order to ask for trust: you have to accept an engineer's decision that what looks like perfectly good bitumen needs resurfacing, so why not trust me in what *I* say?

Turning into the Kerrigan's street he was reminded abruptly of his worsening chances in the Saturday preselection. Mike Prentice lived at the corner and his car was in his driveway.

"Hello, Mr. Order, right on time as usual." Evelyn Kerrigan greeted him warmly. "Come in, come in."

"Bob's not here, but he won't be long," she apologised. "I told him we were expecting you but he decided to slip down to Woden. There's a Big W sale. Shouldn't be more than half an hour. Can I get you a cup of tea?"

"No thanks, Evelyn. How was your trip?"

"Wonderful, Mr. Order," the plump Jenny Fellows-type woman enthused. "Can I show you some of our photos while we wait for Bob? We had them developed as we travelled along."

"D'you mind if we postpone the, er, photographs until another time? Or at least until Bob gets back?"

"Of course not. Sure you won't have some tea?"

"Evelyn, I wonder if I could come back, say in an hour? I'd like to talk to you an' Bob together an' because I've so many people to see before Saturday I could fit in another call now."

"Of course, Mr. Order. You don't need to talk to us anyway; you've got our vote after helping us with those nasty government trees."

Order had no idea what Evelyn Kerrigan was talking about but he knew sometimes you were lucky in politics and were thanked for something you had not done. He recalled the Stop sign episode at Threeways. Accept these freebees without comment, Bernie sensibly had advised, because if the issue comes back later as someone else's help, you can't be accused of lying.

However he had remembered Liz's suggestion he should take the fight for a vote even to his opponent's supporters given the opportunity and if he was in the neighbourhood.

The car of Judas Prentice still was parked in his driveway. Order didn't expect a conversion but he did want to face the bastard and ask why he had switched sides.

As so often when he had been a frequent welcome visitor, the front door was ajar. Order entered and moved left into the familiar lounge room.

Two naked bodies were thrashing about upon the settee. Their raptures nevertheless were not of such high passion that the woman's eyes were closed.

Seeing Order she screamed, or maybe yelped, pushed the man off onto the floor and fled deeper into the house, fumbling to decide which of the sexually interesting three parts of her nude body could be covered by only two hands.

"Ever heard of knocking?" said Prentice, upstanding and struggling into his discarded trousers.

Order grinned at the unintended witticism.

"My office, five o'clock tonight, Mike," he instructed. "Don't bring Lorraine. It'll take her longer than that to get her clothes an' dignity together."

.

TWENTY FOUR

"I can explain, John."

"Close the door, Prentice. Unless you want Liz to hear?"

The visit to the Kerrigan's had been successful. He had had a cup of tea as Evelyn had twice suggested, but was spared the we've-been-travelling photographs by Bob Kerrigan's blunt comment John was a busy man who didn't have time to look at bloody expensive holiday snaps. Order also had time to bring his temper down to a safe heat point.

"How's your wife, Prentice?" he fired as his ex-supporter carefully closed the door.

"Back tomorrow from Sydney, I understand?" he asked in the silence. This from a phone call to Rob Glasson earlier in the afternoon.

Usually Order sat companionably with those who visited his office around the occasional table in surprisingly comfortable government-issue lounge chairs.

Today he remained authoritatively behind his desk, motioning Prentice to either sit upon one such chair some distance from him or draw up a straight backed variety closer to his imposing remoteness.

"One for the road, perhaps?" Order continued unrelentingly. "Before Carol came back?"

He had thought about this confrontation since returning from the Kerrigan's.

Politicians, although they claim to represent the people, live a life completely different from these same people: a life of values, standards and ethics which involves few rules and most behaviour is fair. If you can get away with it fine, if not you suffered the very public consequences.

The notable exception is your private lifestyle, which to their credit even the media was wont to scrupulously respect unless your socially unacceptable behaviour became obviously blatant.

And Order was about to threaten to break this understood code.

Because he'd worked hard, tried to be a good if uninspiring local member, diligent about the often petty but nevertheless important concerns of his constituents. Available twenty four hours a day, seven days a week, involving himself in issues and activities which really did not require the attention of an elected representative. Combining the job of priest, social worker, Mr. Fix-it and bureau-crat and overall, as the old cynical Bob Buchan often said, for an hourly rate which would be rejected by any self-respecting unskilled worker.

"I see how Lorraine gathered votes," he challenged provocatively at Prentice's ongoing silence. "How many did she put out for? An' what will their wives think?"

"It wasn't like that," Prentice finally was goaded to respond.

"So how *was* it?"

"It was a silly lapse of judgment. We'd been working together for weeks. You grow close. Very close. We just lost it an' you caught us. Really that's all there was to it."

Bullshit, thought Order. You're fit, handsome, a lady's man always chatting up women at Party functions. You're wife's out of town, you're randy …

"Why?"

"Why, John? I thought I'd just explained. It was a lapse of judgment -"

"Why did you stop supporting me?"

Prentice looked toward the bookcase behind Order's head and shook his own silently.

"No answer," Order said, adding confidently: "Because you've been bedding Lorraine Bennett behind Bob's back - an' Carol's - for longer than this preselection attempt. That's why."

"Listen John," Prentice began, but Order could see in his ex-friend's eyes he was right.

"No, you listen, Mike." Order's anger softened. For all the worry, the concern, the humiliations he had experienced since the challenge for preselection was mounted, he knew the defiance in defeat Liz understatedly had encouraged now had to be replaced by the magnanimity of victory.

"By noon tomorrow I want a copy of Lorraine Bennett's letter to Bernie withdrawing from the preselection, together with her media release also announcing why. An' I want the media informed tomorrow morning."

"What can she say?" asked an alarmed Prentice.

"No idea, Mike." Friendly again. "I won't say anything but a bland statesmanlike comment, I promise. Assuming I'm asked to comment publicly, of course."

"And if she won't withdraw?"

If he had been asked for what he had wanted from when he first heard of Lorraine Bennett's challenge and the subsequent knowledge he was facing preselection defeat by any means employed by his opponents, Order would have replied as he did so now.

"Then the whole sordid story is leaked to the media, Mike. What a person will do to get preselection. Can't you see the headline? Cost us the seat probably, which won't please the Party. Cost you an' Lorraine your marriages too, I suppose. But perhaps you're in love?"

"You wouldn't dare." But low-key defiance from Mike Prentice. "Anyway, no media would run the story."

"I can give it a go," Order declared. "What have I got to lose if I'm going down in the preselection? Can *you* take that chance?"

"Don't forget, noon tomorrow, Mike," he said before opening the office door and ushering his Judas friend out into a world of unintended consequences.

"Liz?" He stood framed in the doorway to her office, hoping the light heartedness he felt wasn't obvious. "Who's on the visiting list for this evening?"

TWENTY FIVE

Tuesday morning passed slowly.

Using the excuse he was working upon a draft of his preselection speech, Order collected his brag book of media clippings from Liz.

This was a record of published comments, meticulously cut and dated from newspapers, useful to know so you didn't trip up yourself at some future time if publicly addressing the same subject. An indispensable file for all politicians it also worked wonders for the ego.

His own collection was small because he had been in the parliament less than half a term. Most of the collection was from free or throwaway publications: as a backbencher his cautious comments were of little interest to a daily. They always looked for something that broke the party line, which was divisive or embarrassing to the Party itself.

Nevertheless calling it up served his real purpose of keeping Liz out of his office lest his growing impatience and excitement gave away the game. He also asked her to hold *all* telephone calls.

It was a quarter to twelve before she deferentially knocked upon his closed door.

"Sorry to interrupt, John, but I thought this might be important." Liz presented him with a sealed envelope, with no postage and marked urgent and strictly for his attention only.

Now came the difficult part, he realised, of feigning surprise, relief, joy or whatever emotion was produced when the impossibly unexpected happens.

For personal reasons, said the letter and accompanying media release in his hands, Lorraine Bennett had decided to withdraw from Saturday's preselection. She wished to thank her many supporters for their faith in her and their efforts upon her behalf and was sorry to have disappointed their expectations this time.

A simple two paragraph statement. Even the implicit warning was insufficient to dampen a genuine feeling of delight. Expected as it was having the confirmation in his possession was the final assurance.

"Liz! Liz!" He flung open the office door, waving the two sheets of paper. "A miracle!"

"What are the personal reasons?" asked his nevertheless happy secretary, rereading the copy of Lorraine Bennett's surrender.

"They never say, Liz. Family reasons, bankruptcy, bubonic plague, whatever. It doesn't matter, I'm safe."

"You've still to win the seat," Liz said sensibly, bringing him back to earth.

"At least I'll have that chance now."

"Bernie called earlier. I suppose this is what it was about?"

"Probably. I'll phone him back." A thought. "What time?"

"It's on the message slip. About ten-thirty, I think."

Thank God I kept my patience, he thought, when Bernie confirmed a visibly upset challenger had visited him earlier in the day with the letter.

"No reason given?" he probed, because he reasoned it was expected of him.

"None, John. They don't have to, y'know, an' she was so obviously upset I decided it *was* a personal matter. The meeting still goes ahead Saturday of course, because you have to be endorsed, but it's a formality. Congratulations."

Bernie's compliment was the first of many after the midday radio news ran the story.

"Why go to all that effort?" puzzled Rob Glasson over the celebratory late lunch he and Tim Forbes shouted Order in the parliamentary dining room.

The room almost was empty. Order had been busy with media making, as promised, the bland statesmanlike comment prepared for him by Jim Terry. And now he avoided a reply, rising to accept further congratulations from another Government member.

"You know it's about fifty fifty, these nice remarks between ours and theirs," he said, nodding to Jim Rhodes' departing back.

"Because we're all in this together. It's an exclusive club," said Forbes. "Only another member can really know the agony of a preselection challenge or an election fright. Nobody wants to go out of here other than willingly."

"Davenport was in for lunch. She hasn't congratulated you, has she?" asked Glasson, draining his glass of red wine.

"The sisterhood won't be pleased," Forbes confirmed. "They're good haters."

"Let's go. They'll want to clear up." Glasson indicated the hovering staff. "I'd make it up to Selby, John. Send her flowers."

"Yeah, lilies," suggested Forbes, who had had his own disagreements with the Opposition leader's powerful staffer.

The adrenalin of the past fortnight had ebbed away leaving him tired and listless. Order received several more telephone well-wishes during the afternoon, principally from Party supporters and it was not until he was preparing to leave Mrs. Cohen called.

"Mr. Order, I've almost finished the translation," she said, coming straight to the point. "My old brain's memory for Polish is better than I thought. I'd like to see you. I have a favour to ask."

"Of course, Mrs. Cohen. I could come over now."

"No, tomorrow. Tomorrow afternoon if you could. Say two o'clock? I will have finished the translation then."

"Two o'clock then, Mrs. Cohen."

"Those papers I gave you are in a safe place, I trust, Mr. Order?"

"Good," said the old lady upon his assurance, "because as I thought they are very very important."

Early Wednesday morning brought more telephoned congratulations. People who had missed yesterday's radio news but read the In Brief column of the daily newspaper. At his secretary's insistence she continued to contact preselectors to organise meetings.

"Although nobody's interested, John. They can't see the point now."

"They *will* be there on Saturday, Liz?"

"Oh yes. I impressed upon them the importance of ratifying your candidature. Don't want your opposition voting you out."

Fat chance, thought Order, but there was a remote possibility if his own supporters failed to show up and the Bennett camp had a majority they could vote to postpone the candidate selection to a later date.

"I think we should contact all my voters an' the undecided, just to be sure they do turn out next Saturday."

It was slow work, with Liz transferring several of her calls through to him to hear first hand the loyalty they always had had to him. To listen to their unqualified commitment he'd have won in a landslide.

Interrupting this telephonic endorsement Order was sitting in Mrs. Cohen's lounge room shortly after two o'clock accepting several sheets of paper from her bony mottled hands.

"I printed them out for easy reading, Mr. Order. I made a general summary of the official document but the other one spells everything out."

"Indeed it does, Mrs. Cohen," he said, in rising excitement at the understanding of the implications. "Are you sure you've got the right person?"

"Daniel Levy gave a potted family history which he took with him, but I remembered enough. It shouldn't be difficult to check." The old lady handed him another piece of paper with names neatly printed in descending order.

"You said you had a favour of me, Mrs. Cohen?"

"Two actually. To begin with, could you have these papers typed for me?"

"Of course."

"And then see Mr. Conrad for me?"

"I'd be delighted, Mrs. Cohen," Order said with genuine pleasure.

The old lady then gave him very precise instructions about what she wanted, insisted really. She stressed the importance again of the original documents, an opinion Order now so unquestionably shared that upon his return to the parliament he badgered Harold Chambers into retrieving the envelope from his safe and depositing it at his bank.

Liz had typed Mrs. Cohen's translations by the time he returned from the bank and they made extra copies. He marvelled at his secretary's discretion, she said nothing about what she must have read. Not for the first time Order wondered if he *was* so successful in keeping secrets from her.

Thus equipped, he telephoned Conrad.

"I've found the papers," he said brusquely, when the jeweller answered.

"Good. Drop them off at my office today." The tone was neither grateful nor friendly.

Adversity certainly toughened you up, Order decided. "No can do. I need to see you."

"That's not necessary."

"It is." Firmly. This was the bastard who held a cocktail party for my opponent, he reminded himself.

"Just do as you're told!"

"No see, no papers, Conrad. 'Bye."

"Wait." A pause, then Marek Conrad lowered his voice. "I'm in a meeting."

Order imagined him looking out over Lake Burley Griffin from his lofty Kingston office, his back to the minions present.

"Tonight then. My home. Seven sharp."

"Done."

Order thought they probably dead heated hanging up.

TWENTY SIX

It was typical of the arrogance of the man he hadn't bothered to provide an address. He was ex-directory; presumably on the basis those who needed to know where he lived already did so.

A call to a cautious Bernie tracked down the mansion and the security lights blazed as he drove through the entrance gate shared with an adjacent embassy residence.

The chimes were only beginning when the front door opened abruptly. An old white haired man dressed in pyjamas and an open dressing gown stood blinking at him.

"Marek. Good boy. Good boy," he said happily.

The strange spectacle broke up at this point when a white clad figure from behind the opened door took the old man by the arm and wordlessly led him out of sight.

Order moved forward into a large vestibule, closing the door on the cool night air as he did so. His gaze took in expensive-looking occasional chairs, flowers upon stands and paintings upon the walls - one looked like a Nolan - but he had no time to examine anything closely.

"You're here. Let me have them." Conrad dressed for a formal function with a bright stud instead of a black bow tie, imperiously held out his hand.

"Not before you read them," Order said pleasantly and with a smile.

Conrad was about to issue another command when Order added: "I have."

"What d'you mean?" The man was genuinely puzzled.

"Are we going to stand here all night? Because if we are, I'm going home."

"You've got a bloody cheek!"

"And with reason, Mr. Conrad. Now, do we go somewhere more private?"

Grumbling he didn't have time for this, Conrad led him into a comfortable if over furnished room where a cosy fire burned.

Without being asked Order sat upon a white lounge, still holding his small briefcase.

"Don't make yourself comfortable, you're not staying," Conrad said rudely.

Probably where the Bennett's party took place, Order thought, looking around the sizeable space with French windows leading, he guessed, to a side patio. Then he silently removed the papers and had them snatched from his proffered hand.

It took only a second.

"These aren't originals and they're in English," Conrad roared angrily.

"An' make interesting reading."

"What the Hell are you up to Order? I want the originals!"

"I'm sure you do. They're in a very safe place. Trust me."

"I'll not be blackmailed," the jeweller warned, his bulk threatening Order even from a distance.

"I'm sure the police wouldn't do that."

"Police? What the Hell are you talking about?" But the bluster and the angry tone had moderated.

"A young Israeli tourist falls to his death from a hotel balcony after telling an old Jewish lady who survived the Holocaust in Poland that he was here to meet someone called Korzeniowski. How's that for openers?"

"Mistaken identity, I told you. Don't you ever listen?" The confidence was back.

"Daniel Levy didn't think so. He must have spent years checking things out to finally establish the blood line. Like to check it out yourself?" Order offered another piece of paper.

Conrad was about to make another grabbing action when the door was thrust open by a lanky boy with a pimply teenage face. He was dressed in the current youth fashion of a second-hand camouflage battle tunic from the Iraq war years ago, jeans and boots.

"Ever heard of knocking?" Conrad said heatedly.

"Cun' I take the Subaru." A statement rather than a question.

"Where are you going?"

"Out."

I've heard this before, decided Order, and the next answer will be "nothing", but the question was not asked. Conrad simply tossed the gangly youth a set of keys, muttering a warning not to be late.

The interruption did not improve the man's temper.

"I haven't time to waste, Order, and I want the originals." Conrad motioned to suggest his visitor should leave.

"You haven't read the blood line, Conrad. Here. Take it. Look at it." And when the jeweller did not respond but remained standing where he was, his angry eyes wary, Order suggested: "I don't think you're going anywhere in a hurry tonight, Conrad."

"Let me spell out what I've read in the translation then, if you won't bother to face history," Order began.

"According to the documents now in a very safe place and also now translated into English, a Korzeniowski and a Levy were together in the jewellery business in Warsaw in the late 1930's."

"What actually happened, I don't know, but I can guess," continued Order and, irritated by the man's stubborn refusal to accept the seriousness of the situation, broke off the story and snapped: "I suggest you sit down. Otherwise I'll go straight to the police, who doubtless will drag you away from your fancy function

- discretely of course, you being such an important local, indeed, national businessman."

With a weary shake of his head, Conrad threw himself into an armchair.

"These two businessmen sniffed the air from the West and decided it wasn't fresh. They decided it was time to move out but for some reason one - Levy - couldn't do so. Mrs. Cohen thinks his wife might have been an invalid. At least from a childhood an' therefore unreliable memory."

"Anyway, Korzeniowski did leave Poland and shortly afterwards the German's invaded an' Levy's fate was determined."

"But not quite. Like Mrs. Cohen an' her late husband some of the Levy family survived. Most survivors emigrated, seeking new lives but carrying with them the memories of their past. Some even carried more tangible recollections - like documents."

Conrad was looking at the off-white carpet, an expression of indifference upon his face.

"Like the documents Mrs. Cohen has translated, Conrad," Order's temper began to assert itself. "Documents which are agreements between two wealthy jewellers that they would share the spoils of the precious stones they pooled and Korzeniowski took out of Poland."

"The deal, no the agreement, because that's what these documents attest to, was that they would set up in partnership, *together*, somewhere else in the world. One document is the legal arrangement, the second is the personal undertaking signed by both men."

"Who are dead," Conrad said, although quietly.

"Indeed. But what of their offspring, their heirs? Doesn't the agreement hold for them?"

"Why should it?" Defiant.

"Why shouldn't it? Levy thought so. This Korzeniowski got out of Poland with a substantial amount of money, well the equivalent anyway, in diamonds perhaps. He sets himself up on the other side of the world an' waits for his partner - that's the generous interpretation - who never turns up."

"What's that to do with me?"

"Everything. Daniel Levy spent a lot of effort tracking down Korzeniowski and finally decided it was Australia, Canberra in fact. When did your people arrive here?"

"None of your business."

"Then why don't I ask your father?" Order suggested, remembering the front door.

"Or do you let your aged retainers wander through the house in their nightclothes?"

"You've seen my father, Mr. Order," Conrad said confidently. "You'll get nothing out of him."

"Okay. Then the police can find out."

"Why should they?" Defiant again.

"Because a man is dead. A young man who came here to collect what he believed was his family's share of an agreement made over half a century ago. A young man who's death could be suspicious."

"I know nothing about this young man's death. I wasn't even in Canberra."

"How d'you know, Conrad? For someone who denies any knowledge of the incident you're remarkably clear of your whereabouts on the night."

The formal dress was beginning to sag, the stiff white shirt looked crushed and the stud at the throat had lost its glitter.

"Mr. Order, I swear as God is my witness, I wasn't there when Levy fell."

"I was."

TWENTY SEVEN

The voice came from behind Order. A small woman about Marek Conrad's age and well wrapped from the cold stood just inside the French windows.

"Kata. Stay out of this!" Conrad was distressed.

"No, Marek," she said sensibly. "If we're to salvage this situation we can't lie. I'm Marek's sister. I went to see Levy the night he died."

Cherchez la femme, thought Order. No wonder nobody at the hotel remembered a visitor for Levy.

"However, in case you're thinking the obvious, I didn't push him," she concluded.

"Then what happened?" Order asked sternly.

"I don't really know."

She wasn't attractive. A handsome face, helmeted by short black hair. The figure too covered in warm clothes Order noted with disappointment. Even the legs were hidden under dark trousers.

"We discussed what you have suggested. Daniel Levy had documents, well copies, which purported to be legal and personal agreements between our great grandfathers. He said his family was entitled to a share of our financial success. We argued a while, mainly about authenticity - that we were the Korzeniowski's he was looking for - then he started to threaten. Saying how it would make a great story for the newspapers, how we had cheated Jewish survivors of the Holocaust from their rightful share of a legal contract."

"He was very excited. He perched himself on the railing of the balcony and started to demonstrate, by waving his arms out over Canberra, how many people would therefore learn of our - and then he was gone."

"Gone?"

"Yes. Disappeared. He fell off the balcony, Mr. Order."

"Just like that?"

"Just like that. Mr. Levy was a short, thick-set man, twice my weight. You surely don't imagine I could have picked him up and thrown him?" Kata drew herself to her maximum height and confirmed to Order what he already had accepted.

"An' what did you do?"

"What any sensible person would do in such circumstances. I left discretely."

"Taking those copies of the documents you spoke of with you?"

"Of course, along with Levy's mobile"

"But you didn't bargain on Mrs. Cohen?"

"No, we didn't." Marek Conrad rejoined the conversation.

"We didn't know about Mrs. Cohen until she phoned me," the jeweller admitted. "Levy got in touch and we decided someone should see him. I was sceptical. It wouldn't have been the first time someone tried to get money from us. Anyway, Kata thought she should go. A woman's touch?" Conrad's expression was a man-to-man appeal.

"You took a chance."

"We have nothing to hide, Mr. Order," said the woman. "His death was not our fault."

"But you still wanted the originals, so you broke into Mrs. Cohen's home."

"What the Hell are you talking about?" Conrad again was genuinely puzzled.

"Later you went to see Mrs. Cohen," Order continued, "when you couldn't find the papers. You can't deny that. You an' your flash car were seen."

"Correct. For all the good it did me. She didn't understand a word I said."

"Then you'll have a better chance tomorrow."

"Tomorrow?"

"Mrs. Cohen's recovered her senses an' she wants to see you tomorrow."

"I'm a busy man, Order. I haven't time to run around town indulging old lady's whims at short notice. That's your job, you're the politician."

No thanks to you, Order thought grimly, and the memory brought back the rage.

"Please yourself, Conrad." He rose. "Mrs. Cohen's, ten o'clock, otherwise you'll be talking to the police sometime later in the day. Probably the media too."

Kata answered for him. "We don't have any choice, Marek. You must go."

"I'm damned if I'll be blackmailed." Conrad rose to his feet. "This is quite preposterous."

"Then you deny the documents are genuine?" Order hoped this bully would challenge their authenticity.

"It doesn't matter whether or not they are. There's a statute of limitations, I've no doubt."

Again the calm voice of his sister: "We simply can't take the chance. Think, Marek, of the publicity. It won't hurt to see Mrs. Cohen."

This was why Order found himself back in Mrs. Cohen's lounge room the next morning. Conrad had taken a little more persuading but Kata's quiet considered reasoning finally had convinced him there was no choice.

The meeting began uncomfortably. The jeweller, angry and humiliated, objected to Order's presence.

"Mr. Order is here at my insistence, Mr. Conrad," the old lady said, adding primly: "To see justice is done."

Conrad blustered that justice was the last result he could expect from this ridiculous meeting, but Mrs. Cohen cut off his protest.

"A young man came here to seek financial restitution. Now he's dead. The circumstances of his death are open to conjecture. What is not is that he is - was - entitled to a share of his family's fortune."

"Which you think my family owes them," Conrad said flatly but with a sneer, Order thought.

"Yes I do, Mr. Conrad. I can fully understand your bewilderment, anger even, at this unexpected turn of events, but a contract is a contract and must be honoured."

"He's dead."

"But other relatives probably exist. They are entitled -"

"There's no evidence to link my family with this absurd claim."

"Daniel Levy believed there was. He convinced me and I think Mr. Order is convinced too. Of course, we could always put it to the test with a no doubt lengthy and expensive court hearing and, given Daniel's unusual death, involvement of the police."

The room was silent until Conrad with a weary swipe of his shaven head said softly: "I suppose it could all be true."

"We only need to check the records of your family's arrival here from Europe."

"I don't know about that. My grandfather's dead, my great grandfather would have been the person and he's long gone and my father's not fit to remember anything."

"You must appreciate, leaving aside Daniel's death; you haven't committed any crime, Mr. Conrad. You and your family were not to know any Levy survived. At the very worse you're guilty of the sin of omission."

Howso, thought Order.

"You could have searched for them, although in the chaos of Europe …" Mrs. Cohen did not finish the sentence. "To be charitable, I would like to think your great grandfather, and perhaps your grandfather, kept their copies of the documents until there didn't seem to be much point anymore."

In the continuing silence from Conrad, the old lady went on: "You will only create difficulties for yourself and your family from what you do now, not for what happened in the past."

"What do you want?" Conrad capitulated.

"Agreement to a financial settlement for the Levy's, Mr. Conrad. It's complicated because Daniel's dead and we still haven't located next-of-kin in Israel," she glanced at Order who indicated this was so. "I suggest we agree in principle until further information becomes available. Do you agree?" She extended a bony hand.

"And the documents?"

"They remain in a safe place, Mr. Conrad, until we officially seal the bargain."

"It's so open-ended," the jeweller protested. "How much money will I have to find?"

"I've no idea, Mr. Conrad, but I imagine it will be a substantial sum. Your family's had the benefit of the Levy's share for over half a century."

"I'll need time," the man muttered.

"Naturally. With all those years whatever time it takes now hardly matters. Do we have an agreement?"

Wordlessly Conrad finally shook the mottled hand.

"Mr. Order will be my intermediary, Mr. Conrad. And now, if you will both excuse me, I'm very tired." She glanced consolingly at the tablets upon the table beside her.

TWENTY EIGHT

"**E**xtraordinary story, don't you think, Liz?" he said at the end of his account. "Young Levy must have spent years tracking down the Korzeniowski's."

"And then he died so pointlessly."

"An' we still haven't heard from Gabby Williams."

"I don't suggest you contact him again, John. These things take time and we've plenty of that now."

Order worked through until lunch upon accumulated paperwork without enthusiasm, and then drove around most of the afternoon checking out constituents' complaints: a broken street light, graffiti upon a bus shelter, burnouts upon a suburban oval - matters he had unwillingly neglected recently.

So many politicians are only interested in the big picture, Bernie once had told him, and they forget it's the little day-to-day issues which win the votes to get them elected. Roads, rates and rubbish, John, are the foundation of a successful parliamentary career.

That night he followed more of Bernie's sage advice and attended another but non-contentious local monthly community meeting. He had no especial reason to be present but occasionally went along to one of them, sitting quietly in the middle of the room in the middle of the audience, showing the flag, making himself available, listening to the electorate's concerns - the chair aware of his presence upon such occasions. It was relaxing to be able to do so after the stressful events of the past three weeks, particularly without the threat of Lorraine Bennett's aggressive attendance.

How little time we allow ourselves as politicians to think, he realised, listening to a string of unoriginal and wildly expensive suggestions to improve a rubbish strewn block of vacant land. Snowed under with reading or letters to sign or parliamentary meetings to attend, we abdicate the crucial responsibilities to our constituents to our minders, people who have no direct obligation to the electorate except in the abstract of how to win or how to retain victory.

He thought how fortunate he was to have Liz, dedicated and discreet. Virtues he easily could have recalled the next morning when he arrived late at the office.

The wind was fresh. Each day it seemed to be a fraction cooler, no matter if the official temperature reading did not vary.

Order was taking off his overcoat when his secretary handed him the message slip and returned to her own room.

With the pre-selection resolved in his favour and Conrad compliant, he'd forgotten the third component of his problem trifecta. Nevertheless he tried to sound convincing.

"Rabbit. How are you? I was worried."

"That I doubt. You'd have guessed if I hadn't been in touch *we* had nothing to worry about."

She sounded as cool as the weather outside, Order thought, memories of their previous lustful encounters stirring his feelings. I'll have to work on this.

"That's true, but I was concerned all the same," he lied.

"I'll bet. Anyway, the scare set me thinking, so I talked with David."

He waited. The earlier sensation turning to alarm.

"I'm going to join him in Sydney. Permanently. The southern highlands are the same distance from there as from here so we can see the children as regularly. Last weekend we found a house and I'm moving tomorrow. It's stupid to keep two residences."

"Your job?" Order hoped his voice didn't sound weak with relief.

"A simple transfer." Rabbit paused. "I thought I'd better tell you."

"I'll miss you, Rabbit." This *was* genuine.

"No you won't, John. Only the sex and you'll soon replace me in that."

We had a lot of fun; he was preparing to say, when she added: "Congratulations, by the way. Thank you and goodbye, John."

Beaten again to the disconnection, Order slowly replaced the receiver. At least she closed off friendlier.

"Gabby's on the line," Liz called through, as he struggled with new feelings.

"Gabby. News at last?"

"No an' yes. Nothing from Israel. I'm at Mrs. Cohen's."

"Whatever for?"

"She's dead."

The street looked unusually empty for such a big event. One squad car and another vehicle were parked in front of the house as Order crossed quickly to the front door.

Gabby Williams stood in the familiar lounge room. A big man with sleepy patient eyes he was flanked by a younger offsider Order thought he recognised.

"Sergeant Shanks," said the detective inspector, nodding in the man's direction, and Order remembered Ted Shanks. He was as laconic as his boss.

"What happened? Where is she?"

"Gone already. Heart attack, I'd say."

Seeing Order's puzzled expression Williams consented to say a little more.

"Found by a friend who phoned us. I remembered your involvement."

"Then where's Mrs. Bennett?"

"Who's she?"

Shanks opened his notebook.

"Her neighbour across the street. Didn't she find her?"

"No. A lady from the Jewish Centre. She's in the kitchen with a policewoman."

"I decided to come over, John, even though it's straightforward, and I thought I'd call you to fill in the details."

"What details?"

"You were helping her with the boy's death, weren't you?"

"Yes." Order thought quickly. "He left her – Mrs. Cohen - some papers. They were in Polish an' she translated them an' I had them typed up for her."

"Papers? We find any papers?" Gabby said, not even looking at Shanks.

"No papers."

"Probably put away. When did you last see the deceased?"

"Yesterday morning."

"About the papers?"

"Yes." It wasn't a lie.

"What were they about?"

"Old historical documents, I believe." Again true. "I didn't read them, none of my business." Porky time and his turn for a question.

"You say it was a heart attack?"

"Appears so. She was in hospital recently, wasn't she? That's what the lady who found her told us. Said she had a heart condition."

"That's true. Mrs. Cohen took tablets -"

"Where are the tablets?" he asked the policeman, his eyes upon the bare occasional table.

"Sergeant?"

"No tablets," confirmed Shanks.

TWENTY NINE

Order slowly drove back to the office, needing time to think. Detective Inspector Williams didn't seem too concerned about Mrs. Cohen's missing heart tablets nor the papers.

"We'll probably find them somewhere in the house," he said dismissively.

A few more perfunctory questions and Order was free to leave. The only new piece of information, very much subject to official examination, was the old lady had died in the past twenty four hours.

"Plenty of scope, Liz," he said to his secretary.

"Did you tell them about Conrad?"

"No." The same question had troubled him on the way back to the parliament.

"Was that wise?"

"Don't know. The absence of the tablets is puzzling, but hardly cause for suspicion. As Gabby said they could be somewhere else, the bedroom for example. An' if I tell the police what the documents were all about, coupled with Levy's death -"

"They might jump to conclusions?"

"Exactly. Mrs. Cohen's death may be an unfortunate coincidence, possibly brought on by recent events."

"But no grounds to accuse Conrad?"

"Exactly again. I think I'll sit tight an' see what happens."

"And work on your preselection speech while you're waiting."

Order's desk was covered with scraps of paper: notes and ideas he was attempting to fit together into a coherent continuous address, when late in the afternoon DI Williams' telephoned.

"You mentioned tablets," he began in his usual blunt style. "Tell me about them."

"Nothing to tell, except Lydia – Mrs. Cohen - was never without them."

"Bottle? Plastic container? Big? Small? Colour perhaps?"

"Small plastic container. White, I recall. She took them with water."

Gabby's silence prompted him.

"Didn't you find them or the papers?"

"No, John. Despite a thorough search."

"So what now?"

"We continue our enquiries. Cause of death will probably clear it up, if it's a heart attack."

"Howso?"

"Ran out of pills."

"Keep me advised, please," Order said quickly before the line was disconnected.

It was darkening outside, the traffic building up for the thirty minute Canberra evening rush hour. Order hoped Conrad was in town.

"What do you want now, Order?" The tone was unfriendly.

"To see you, Conrad. Tonight."

Anger drove him but he couldn't see any fair alternative, much as he disliked the man.

"Well, I don't want to see you."

"Mrs. Cohen's dead, Conrad. Suspicious circumstances," he added, before the jeweller could hang up as he imagined he was going to do.

"What the Hell are you driving at?"

"Just what I said. Tonight. Me or the police?"

"I had nothing to do with it."

A statement he repeated forcefully in the comfortable over-furnished lounge room of two nights ago. Conrad himself had opened the main door and led him silently to the room where Kata awaited them.

Order ignored the denial and briefly explained the circumstances as he knew them of Mrs. Cohen's death.

"The police believe she died sometime in the twenty four hours before she was found this morning an' her heart tablets are missing," he concluded.

"So?"

How much aggression can you express in such a short word, Order marvelled, before taking the dangerous plunge.

"So have you an alibi for those twenty four hours?" he asked, reasonably he hoped.

"How dare you come into my home and accuse me -" Conrad, red faced, had risen and was advancing menacingly across the off-white carpet, his fists clenched and rising up his body.

"Marek no! Stop! Think!" Kata blocked her brother's progress.

Order himself had got to his feet; the better to protect himself, and now added his persuasion to Kata's entreaties.

"It's a fair question, Conrad, an' one the police certainly will ask."

"Marek, sit down. Hear this man out." Kata pushed Conrad back and into his chair.

"I haven't mentioned your involvement - yet." But I will if you keep up this threatening performance, he thought. "Because if Mrs. Cohen died from natural causes, there's no need."

"She's dead." The jeweller shrugged. "What's it matter?"

Order's anger reasserted itself. "The missing tablets," you miserable bastard, he managed to check himself from adding. "Mrs. Cohen has evidence your family owed the Levy's a substantial amount of money - no, shut up 'til I finish - amassed over half a century. The original documents prove there was an agreement an' it was going to cost you plenty to pay out the partner's heirs. Mrs.

Cohen had a heart condition, which you know about because she's been in hospital an' you sent her flowers, remember?"

"An' you visited her at home too," he continued, "because her neighbour Mrs. Bennett saw you."

"Then she dies after making demands upon your business an' now the documents an' the heart tablets can't be found. You see how nasty minds might think you decided there was another way? You could be in the frame, as they say, Conrad."

"I was in the office all day and home with my wife all night."

"Can she vouch for that?"

"My wife is an invalid, Order, but I don't spend my spare time at her bedside holding hands. I was in my study working."

"Anyone else who can vouch for that? Your father? The nurse?"

"My father's in respite for a few days, not that he could vouch for anything. The nurse has taken the time off." Conrad's temper had subsided. He was speaking slowly, thoughtfully, now aware of the ramifications for him of the old lady's sudden death.

"I made a few phone calls."

"They won't stand up. Could be from anywhere, especially if you used your mobile."

Conrad's expression of concern saved the answer and Order turned enquiringly to the diminutive Kata.

"I was out at a bridge evening. It takes four to play," she said helpfully.

"But what about you, *Mister* Order," the jeweller suddenly rallied, accentuating the honorific. "You're - were – Mrs. Cohen's interme-diary, wasn't it? Don't you need an alibi too?"

"Howso?"

"You're the only person still living directly involved is why *and* you know where the originals of the documents are." It was Order's turn to silently betray the answer. "Why not a double cross perhaps? Siphon off a handsome commission from the unsuspecting Israeli relatives? Where were *you* yesterday?"

"I was at a meeting last night." For Kata's benefit: "Plenty of people."

"And during the day? You said she'd been dead up to twenty four hours."

"Travelling around the electorate."

"Travelling around the electorate," an increasingly confident Conrad repeated. "Catching up on neglected constituency work, no doubt. See anyone?"

"Not that I recall," Order admitted uncomfortably.

"So your alibi's no better than mine. You could easily have gone back to Mrs. Cohen's, nobody would have thought it strange, you've been there often enough."

"An' where was your son?" Order countered, making a guess about another apparition from the previous visit.

"Jan?" Conrad's face grew red again. "You leave him out of this."

"Why? Doesn't he need an alibi? He's old enough to drive."

"Marek?" Kata's question was marked with concern upon her face.

"Out with his friends, I suppose," his father muttered unconvincingly.

"You'd better find out." Order wondered if he'd mistaken concern for guilt in Kata's expression.

"And you'd better get out of here now. Before I lose my temper."

Order drove home, frequently checking the rear mirror.

THIRTY

"**G**abby. Any news?" There had been some fog or mist this morning, heralding a sunny day, and in spite of his doubts Order was feeling at peace with the world when the policeman telephoned.

"Heart attack, as we thought."

"And?"

"And nothing. We'll make a few more routine enquiries, that's all."

"I'm glad you called. I've a favour to ask. Constituency matter," Order lied.

"Depends." Guarded now.

"A boy. Well, youth. About seventeen or eighteen."

"That's about ten percent of the population. Have a name?"

"Jan Conrad. I want to know if he's come to official attention."

"Why?"

"Mother's worried he might be mixing with the wrong crowd. You know how it is," he added, sure Williams probably did. Then Order had an inspiration: "I'm looking for part-time help here in the office," he lied again, "but I don't want to take on a delinquent."

"I'll see, John."

Order worked diligently but unsuccessfully upon his preselection speech throughout the day. It just didn't jell.

A quick sandwich, with the usual repetitive ordering confirmations from makers who didn't listen, to avoid breaking his train of thought by an enjoyable wet lunch with Glasson and Forbes did nothing to improve his thought processes.

He simply could not get the construction right.

Politicians understood it was the rank and file Party members to whom he was now appealing for endorsement who were the problem. Always hating their political opponents with fanatical zeal.

Yet Order did not see it in such uncomplicated terms and he was keen to illustrate that the differences in political opinion or philosophy were not substantial. For example, care for the poor depended upon the taxes of the rich, while the profits of the rich depended upon the support of the poor. Or was this too simplistic for a rabid pre-selection committee?

And then there was Bernie's aphorism which held politicians and supporters fundamentally were only interested in the next election and not the long-term future. Politics is about power *now* not history's judgment, was the old Party secretary's conviction.

Order wondered if he was trying too hard to impress. As a tyro who had been in less than half of the parliamentary term and holding by 176 votes, he was desperate to prove himself. You can't measure the boost winning your seat for a second time gives to a politician's confidence, Bernie had assured him during one of his despondent periods in the past.

The president of the Party's electoral division telephoned to see if he was ready to face the preselectors tomorrow.

"Ready as I ever will be, Craig. 'Though I'm puzzled why we're bothering as I'm unopposed."

"The admin committee considered that, John, and we decided to go through with it because a challenge had been made. Members have the option to reject a candidate, you know."

Order wondered how a Vietnam veteran who had lost his right arm managed the telephone.

"Not that I think you'll face that difficulty. Anyway, we didn't want the expense of contacting everyone to say the preselection was off and it's good public relations, all fair and aboveboard."

Shortly after Craig Hudson's call, Liz formally announced the arrival of visitors.

"Detective Inspector Williams and Sergeant Shanks, Mr. Order."

"Unexpected but welcomed, Gabby. You really didn't have to come in person," Order began.

"We did, as it happens," was all the policeman replied.

"So, what have you got for me?" Order was pleased to be away from wrestling with the speech.

"Jan Conrad's a bit of a tearaway. Nothing indictable but he's been cautioned a few times for bad behaviour in public, a few speeding tickets, a couple of burnouts - 'though nothing proven - and we suspect the usual graffiti vandalism. Well, unusual graffiti."

"Unusual?"

"Yeah. If he's to blame. He's a racist."

"Racist?"

"Yes. Arabs, Asians, you name it."

"Jews?"

"Of course. I said he's a racist, if we can ever prove it."

"Well, thanks, Gabby. I'll obviously have to rethink my employment offer," said Order, sticking to his original lie.

"That's not why we're here," said Williams seriously. "Why didn't you tell us you saw the late Mrs. Cohen Wednesday afternoon?"

"Because I didn't."

"We have a neighbour who says you did. Says she recognises your car from frequent visits to Mrs. Cohen's."

"Mrs. Bennett?"

"Whomever, but a good guess. Well?"

"I swear I haven't been near Mrs. Cohen's since we talked together Wednesday morning."

"You sure?" There was no friendliness now in Gabby Williams' question nor in his expression and Sergeant Shanks was taking down the conversation verbatim.

"Positive."

"Very well, Mr. Order, we'll leave it for the moment." DI Williams rose. "You're not planning to leave town, I trust?"

"No. Gabby, what's all this about? Am I a suspect? Did you find the heart tablets and the papers?"

"No, Mr. Order," said the policeman, leaving him to decide which question was being answered.

"What *were* you doing Wednesday afternoon?"

"Out in the electorate chasing up local complaints."

"I'd like a list of your movements," the detective inspector said from the doorway. "And who you saw."

Order's immediate reaction was to contact Mrs. Bennett. In fact he'd picked up the receiver when he realised a telephone call wouldn't tell him what he wanted to know. He needed to see her face to face.

As he prepared to leave, again he checked his movement.

Another visit to the street would only add to existing suspicions and Mrs. Bennett would be sure to report it to the police.

It could be an innocent mistake, of course, there must be dozens of white Camry sedans in Canberra. But unlikely.

Unless someone had got to the old nurse. She probably could do with the money, he reasoned. And it wouldn't do any real harm, only muddy the water; he could hear her plausible justification, because Mr. Order would have an alibi.

Unless again, you knew he hadn't.

"Mr. Conrad's not available, sir," said the receptionist, politely but firmly.

"He'll talk to me. John Order." he insisted.

"He's interstate, sir. Can anyone else help you?"

"His sister," he gambled and was pleased at his successful punt when asked to wait.

Self-congratulation turned to mild concern when he realised he didn't know her real name.

"John Order," he announced.

"Kata Conrad, Mr. Order," the quiet voice confirmed. "Can I help you? Marek's in Melbourne."

"I need to talk to him - both of you. An' knowing his reluctance to have anything to do with me, please pass on that his efforts with Mrs. Bennett will only delay nailing his tearaway son. Do you understand?"

"We will get back to you, Mr. Order."

The Party meeting the next afternoon found Order in a mild panic because he remained unprepared for his preselection address. The implications of Mrs. Bennett's lie to the police had distracted him from planning his speech, so it remained the random collection of notes which had been scattered across his office desk on Thursday.

Now he stood with the one armed chairman nodding with a tight smile to the pre-selection delegates as they moved into the meeting room.

Order had dressed carefully. A dark single breasted suit, white shirt and neutral colour coordinated tie. He was in contrast to most of the members, many of whom looked as if they had come straight from the chilly playing fields of children's Saturday morning sport.

At least he was confident in his dress. People in a city which prided itself upon its egalitarianism for some strange reason wanted their representatives to look a cut above them. Some indeed would have been threateningly offended if he had turned up in joggers, skivvy and anorak.

"Five minutes to go," announced Craig Hudson. "How many have we, Bernie?"

The Party secretary had made the ultimate sacrifice for a chain smoker and was handling the pre-selection vetting himself: checking off the names of those members who were financial and had attended the required number of branch meetings to be entitled to vote. Despite the absence of a cigarette Order's nose twitched from the old man's smoke saturated clothes.

"Forty one of a possible fifty four," he intoned.

The Warbergs hadn't shown, Order noted, probably watching their bloody AFL match. Neither had his parliamentary colleague Paul Severin, which meant he wasn't committed to the old Tory's anti-graffiti proposal. And nor had Prentice and the Bennett's.

"I'd better get this rolling," said the president, who was chairing the meeting. "Don't want to be here all day. You know the drill, John, ten minute speech *maximum*," he stressed, "then ten minutes of questions. Okay? Tom," he nodded to the doorman, "will tell you when we're ready. Good luck."

And just before the door closed, Liz arrived with Jayson. Although unable to vote they could sit in as observers and he was heartened by his secretary's friendly wink.

It always was the waiting which placed the greatest stress upon candidates, political aspirants claimed. Once you were at the podium staring above a mass of serious unidentifiable faces to a spot somewhere on the back wall, you were committed.

Remember, the wise old Bernie often had assured him, he who has the microphone controls the meeting.

Without preparation Order was hard pressed to remember what he said.

Essentially Liz told him later he outlined how he'd become the local member, the work he'd put in since - a modest comment this - a few initiatives he had taken like the regular electorate newsletter and how, if the preselectors would grant him the honour, he would like to continue as their candidate, confident with their help the position again would translate into also being their parliamentary representative and in government following the next election.

His speech lasted seven minutes, again according to Liz. An acceptable length which avoided the amateur's mistake of taking the full time available and repeating oneself.

For the question time he adopted the politician's ploy when faced with a time limit of giving long and detailed replies. Thus he fielded only four of which one, about his bachelor status asked by Bennett supporter Steve Spencer, gave him any concern, although Liz thought the question impertinent and probably did more harm to the person asking it than to Order.

A vote was taken after he had withdrawn from the room. It gave him a handsome re-endorsement: thirty four to six with a mysterious one informal.

Over a celebratory drink at Manuka with Liz and a very impressed Jayson, Order wondered who had not voted.

"We'll never know," said Liz, sipping from a glass of red wine. "And does it matter?

"Probably couldn't work out what to do." She laughed. "Or maybe thought you had something to hide."

Bankruptcy, being of unsound mind, holding another office of profit or convicted of an offence carrying a jail term of five years or more, could remove even an elected politician from office, far less a candidate.

The knowledge soured the victory.

THIRTY ONE

"**G**ood weekend?" asked Liz on Monday morning when he arrived late.

"Yes. Did nothing after Saturday."

"Do you good for a change. Media bother you?"

"No. Jim Terry issued a statement on the result but I don't think anyone ran it. Not contentious."

"Rob Glasson and Tim Forbes want to take you to lunch and Mrs. Wilberforce phoned to say she was rejoining the Party now you've won preselection."

"Until next time."

"Said she'd vote for you."

"She would anyway. Nobody else phoned?"

Conrad's silence unsettled Order, who remembered the previous occasion the jeweller hadn't bothered to contact him. So the day passed slowly, even several congratulatory telephone calls and a good lunch with his political friends did not lift his spirits.

He was moodily tossing up whether to confront Mrs. Bennett or to try to speak with Conrad again when Liz announced Les Preen's arrival.

"He insists on seeing you, John," his secretary whispered, indicating the fat intriguer was waiting outside. "Probably wants to congratulate you."

"Hello, Les," he said without grace. "What can I do for you?"

"That depends," said Preen in an unfriendly tone. "Congratulations, by the way."

"Thanks."

Preen was not his volatile self, Order noted. Usually full of gossip or stirring up trouble for someone, he stood uneasily in front of Order's desk, gazing out of the window at the leaves blowing spasmodically from the trees.

"Marek Conrad sent me," he finally blurted out. "It's about his son, Jan."

"How d'you know Conrad?"

"I just do. Look, can I sit down?"

Order joined him at the visitors' round table, perplexed but still not encouraging a conversation.

"Marek reckons you think Jan killed an old lady who was causing his father trouble and you're threatening him."

"No more than he's threatening me," Order replied grimly, thinking of the probable bribe and Mrs. Bennett's claim to the police.

"And I'm here to tell you you're wrong, John. Whatever happened had nothing to do with Jan Conrad."

"Howso?"

"Because he has an alibi -"

"For twenty four hours?"

"That's right."

"Okay, Les. Let's hear it."

"Jan Conrad is a problem youth. Nothing too bad. Speeding, drunk in public, vandalism, a few brawls, maybe petty theft – although God knows why with the money they've got. He's been cautioned a few times by the police and Marek's paid any fines and managed to hush up these matters."

"Sounds just like the person we're looking for an' you left out break an' enter."

"I wouldn't know about that," Preen looked genuinely surprised. "Anyway, the alibi is that he goes to a special school for troubled youth," he mentioned a well-known community group. "It's out-of-town and he's there from nine until three every day *or else*."

"That doesn't explain Wednesday night," Order said coldly, as Preen settled back more confidently in his chair. "The police said twenty four hours maximum. Mrs. Cohen could have died later in the day."

"He still couldn't have done it," the man said emphatically.

"Why?"

"John, can I have your word this will go no further?"

"Depends." But he was shocked by the entreaty in the gossip's tone.

"Because he was with my son."

The admission seemed to come as a relief and Preen hurriedly continued: "They're mates. They both go to the special school then pal up at night. He was with Andrew Wednesday night."

"Doing what?" But Order's own tone had softened, aware of the effort Preen, the trouble maker, the supreme political intriguer, had made. Aware too of the resignation and defeat in his visitor's voice.

"How would I know? You're single, John. You've no idea how difficult, impossible even, it is to get a teenager to tell you anything if they don't want to."

"Andrew got in about midnight. I found spray cans in the car next morning, so I'd guess they were scribbling graffiti somewhere."

Heaven help you if Paul Severin ever finds out, Order thought irrationally.

"Jan Conrad could have gone over to Mrs. Cohen's afterwards, Les."

"No. Andrew dropped him home. They had our car Wednesday night."

"Still possible."

"Marek said he could hardly stand. Bourbon and coke, I think."

"Les are you willing to swear to this in court?"

"If I have to." Fear came into his eyes. "But I hope it won't come to that."

And Order didn't know whether or not to agree with him, so he thanked his chastened colleague and promised to keep the information to himself.

"What do I tell Marek?" Preen asked anxiously.

"My promise holds for him too, but tell him the other matter remains unresolved an' needs sorting out."

"I don't know what you mean. What other matter?"

"Conrad will know. Just tell him."

Showing Preen to the door, Order closed it behind him then sprawled in his desk chair. The falling leaves outside the window reminded him the tree would soon be bare, like his political future and his reputation.

Conrad had trapped him neatly. Knowing his son could not have killed Mrs. Cohen, he'd bribed Mrs. Bennett to tell the police about Order's fictitious Wednesday afternoon visit. With his own alibi for Wednesday night unable to be substantiated, Marek Conrad had taken advantage of Order's own lack of proof that he had spent the afternoon driving around the electorate upon constituency business.

With one stroke he'd diverted attention from himself. Order now was in the frame.

And if he was in any doubt, Gabby Williams' second unannounced visit Tuesday morning confirmed it.

"Mr. Order," the detective inspector began, beside him sat Sergeant Shanks, pen and notebook ready. "You were the last person to see Mrs. Cohen alive, Wednesday afternoon. D'you have anything more to tell us?"

"No. I didn't visit her in the afternoon, Inspector."

"I needn't tell you how serious this situation is. We're checking the local pharmacies and if we establish the old lady had an adequate supply of heart tablets - missing tablets - we may have to take you in for questioning."

Why haven't you, thought Order.

"I appreciate we have a sensitive situation, Mr. Order. We

certainly don't want to jeopardise your position, but we must act as we see fit if the evidence …"

"I understand," Order said when the policeman let his remarks hang in the quiet office air.

"D'you have the list of your movements and the people you saw?"

"I have the list but I didn't see anyone an' nobody saw me that I know of. I don't always visit people, just places, Inspector. It saves time."

"I see."

Williams passed the typed paper to Shanks without looking at it and stood.

"Don't leave town, Mr. Order," he commanded, and the two policemen made their way to the door.

Order tried unsuccessfully several times to telephone Marek Conrad but the man was resolutely unavailable and from the increasingly cool response of the receptionist it was obvious he did not want to speak to him. Kata simply was out.

With another pre-budget committee hearing fast approaching, Order telephoned Les Preen.

"He's out all day, Mr. Order," explained his secretary. "The environment committee's looking at the Pialligo wetlands. Back about four or four thirty."

He allowed Wendy Wonder to take the running in questioning the earnest community groups appearing before them, hardly aware of who was who or what they wanted. Even the chairman, Jim Rhodes, cast him several puzzled glances, so deep was his preoccupation.

It looked like a lonely worrying afternoon until coming back from the shredder shortly before three o'clock he passed in the corridor Sean Seymour, a young idealistic cross bench member, who was wearing heavy clothing.

Back in his office Order checked his committee membership list.

"Yes, he's back, Mr. Order -"

"Put him on please. It's urgent."

"I was going to ring you, John," apologised Preen.

"I want to see you, Les. Now! It's urgent."

"I've only just got back. My desk -"

"Les, I said *now*. Imagine what Paul Severin would make of a graffiti artist so close to the Opposition."

Preen suggested Order's parents had never been married, but he was in the office shortly afterwards.

"What did Conrad say?" he forestalled the man, closing the door behind him.

"That he wants nothing more to do with you - ever." Preen stood, hunched in a windcheater, corduroy trousers and heavy muddy boots. "Can I go now and get changed?"

"No. What about the other matter?"

"He said he didn't know what you're talking about."

"Here." Order motioned to the telephone. "Ring him."

"What for?" Preen looked uncomfortable.

"Conrad won't speak to me but I'm hoping he'll speak to you. I'm going to take you into my confidence, Les, so you can spell out clearly to your mate just what I'm on about."

"Jesus," said Preen, his discomfort replaced with alarm after Order had explained his predicament and Marek Conrad's role in Mrs. Bennett's lie. "That's a serious allegation, Order."

"Just do it, Les. Make the call. I've nothing to lose, but you still have."

He watched glumly as Preen dialled, was predictably put through and, careful to mention Order was present and had required him to make the telephone call, explained the other matter.

Preen's deferential tone abruptly altered and he passed the receiver to Order.

"He wants to speak to you," he whispered.

"Order here," with all the confidence he could muster.

"Mr. Order, I thought you should hear this from me rather than second-hand. Upon my word I've never spoken to nor seen your Mrs. Bennett. I've also never bribed anyone in my life and I look forward to suing you if you make this slanderous accusation public."

And Order again was holding a disconnected telephone receiver.

THIRTY TWO

Les Preen gratefully made his escape and Order went home shortly afterwards, where he spent a quiet night thinking, fortified by several glasses of white wine.

Next morning a blustery cool wind from the Brindabella Ranges and further south, the Snowy Mountains, propelled him to his bank where he withdrew from the safe deposit what he had come to know as the Cohen documents.

Back at his office a long argumentative telephone conversation with DI Williams resolved in his favour, Order packed his briefcase and cancelled the morning's two constituency appointments.

At ten forty five he was knocking upon the door, accompanied by an obviously uneasy policeman.

"Mr. Order?" Mrs. Bennett's eyes shared William's discomfort.

"You know Detective Inspector Williams, Mrs. Bennett?" And before she could reply: "May we come in?"

"I'm just going out."

"We won't keep you long," Order said implacably.

"It's not very tidy." Mrs. Bennett was flustered, embarrassed Order thought, as would be anyone face to face with a person they'd lied about. But she stood aside.

"Mrs. Bennett," Order began when they were all seated upon the tattered pieces of the lounge suite. "You made certain accusations - serious accusations - to the police about me being at Mrs. Cohen's house Wednesday afternoon the day she died. Why did you do so?"

"Because it's true."

"What was I wearing, Mrs. Bennett?"

"Well, a suit I suppose. Yes, a suit," she repeated with greater conviction.

"What colour?"

"Grey. Yes, grey I think. My eyes -"

"Aren't too good? Then how did you know my suit was grey?"

"It was you, Mr. Order. I recognised your car."

"My car? How could you be sure it was *my* car? There are many white Camry's in Canberra, yet you say it was *my* car an' your eyes aren't too good."

"Officer, are you going to let Mr. Order browbeat an old woman into making mistakes about what I saw?"

"Mrs. Bennett, Mr. Order could be facing a serious charge upon your evidence."

Nevertheless Williams shifted uncomfortably on the lounge chair. He knows we shouldn't be doing this, decided Order. We'll be crucified if it ever gets up in court.

"Mrs. Bennett, I wasn't wearing a grey suit Wednesday an' there are people who can testify to the fact. As to my car, it could have been anyone."

"I've got to go," Mrs. Bennett protested.

"Then I'll come to the point."

But at that very point he couldn't do so, because the front door opened and Sergeant Shanks' head cautiously looked in.

"Sergeant Shanks! Am I happy to see you," exclaimed Mrs. Bennett. "Come in, please."

Shanks ignored her and nodded briefly to an expectantly watchful Williams.

"Mrs. Bennett," continued Order, disregarding the interruption but noting Shanks, seeing all seats were taken except on the lounge beside the old nurse, elected to stand. "Originally I thought you'd been bribed to lie about Wednesday afternoon, but I no longer think so. So now your lie has been exposed we have to find another reason."

Order lifted and opened his briefcase, removing the Cohen documents.

"Remember these, Mrs. Bennett? You gave them to me after Mrs. Cohen came out of hospital?"

"Yes, of course I remember. I forgot I had them after Lydia had her heart attack."

"Bit bulky aren't they? Reasonable size too, particularly as a doubled over A4 envelope."

"So? I don't understand you, Mr. Order."

"You don't really want to, Mrs. Bennett, because you didn't find something this size under Mrs. Cohen's body the day she had her heart attack. You didn't have this envelope *at that time*."

"Are you going to let this man accuse me of lying?" Mrs. Bennett appealed, to a response which would have done proud a couple of Easter Island moai.

"Remember the break-in, Mrs. Bennett? I found it odd when we looked around. Most burglaries are messy affairs; the house turned upside down, a hurried destructive search. People claim they feel violated. Or else it's done very carefully, so you don't even know your jewellery's missing until you need it. At least those are the two alternative scenarios constituents have explained to me when they're complaining about police inaction." He directed a depreciatory smile at DI Williams, who nodded. Encouragement? Agreement? Order plunged on.

"It looked amateurish. Drawers just pulled out, items rifled through. Like someone who wanted to make it look like a break-in but respected property too much to make a mess. A woman perhaps who understood the personal nature of old people's belongings. And certainly someone who was searching for something specific."

"An' the break-in itself. The back door lock in so many of these old properties is a flimsy affair, easily broken. Privacy to do the deed was also guaranteed by the sheltered back porch. I'll bet we can find a heavy implement, a hammer perhaps, even an old lady could use to make an entry - or at least create that impression."

"I insist you leave immediately or I'll call -"

"They're here, Mrs. Bennett, an' on a far more important matter." Order paused.

"Murder," he said.

"You can't be serious." Mrs. Bennett's eyes were wide with shock.

"You broke into Mrs. Cohen's house - well, made out someone did - an' stole the documents for reasons yet to be established. Mrs. Cohen subsequently dies an' her heart tablets are missing. You then lie about seeing me at her house during the twenty four hours over which she died, again for reasons - well, it's becoming clear. There's one constant, Mrs. Bennett. *You had a key*."

"This is silly. I'm not going to listen to this anymore. I'm asking you all to leave." Mrs. Bennett rose and began moving toward the door.

"Sit down, Mrs. Bennett!" snapped Williams and Shanks stepped aside to block the front exit.

"Shanks?" the DI asked.

"Mr. Bailey, Mrs. Cohen's next door neighbour, confirms Mrs. Bennett made regular visits to Mrs. Cohen's house," the sergeant began.

"We were friends," Mrs. Bennett interrupted.

"Including when she was in hospital," Shanks concluded.

"Mr. Bailey's a grumpy dirty old man. He asked me to sleep with him once. I refused, of course, so he hates me."

"Access, opportunity, motive yet to be established," said Williams.

"Tablets?" queried Order.

Williams gave him a stay-out-of-this frown. "We'd like to search your house, Mrs. Bennett."

Forestalling her, he added: "I have a warrant."

"Try the handbag," Order suggested helpfully, nodding to the item beside the lounge.

Shanks, now wearing white surgical gloves because it belonged to a suspect, fossicked delicately into the recesses of the woman's bag.

"Tablets," he announced.

THIRTY THREE

It was an irrelevant thought, but in the silence following Shanks' discovery, Order wished there was a grandfather clock to imperturbably tick away.

Instead, Williams said: "Now we have the tablets it will be a simple matter to establish with what regularity they had to be taken, Mrs. Bennett."

"They're mine," she claimed.

Shanks shook his head.

"Prescription in Mrs. Cohen's name and you're a nurse," Williams continued. "You'd better get your coat, Mrs. Bennett."

"Why did you do it?" Order asked.

"This is police business, John," intervened Gabby Williams, forgetting formalities. "We'll continue in Civic."

"I'm involved. I'm entitled to some answers. What I want hasn't anything to do with the murder."

"I didn't kill Mrs. Cohen," Mrs. Bennett wailed. "She was dead when I found her."

"Then why steal the documents an' the tablets an' lie about me?"

"John, I insist! Be quiet, Mrs. Bennett."

"No. I don't know anything about the documents. I never saw them 'til I gave them to you and we looked at them together, Mr. Order."

I'm guessing here, decided Order, but here goes.

"You're lying. I think Mrs. Cohen confided in you, Mrs. Bennett.

You were friends, you visited her often. She was a lonely old lady," with many memories, he thought. "It's natural she'd want to share with someone such exciting information provided by Levy's visit. I think she told you she was given some papers for safekeeping. Papers that could be worth a lot of money perhaps."

"Mrs. Bennett, this is just speculation -" began Williams.

"No, Mr. Order's right," Mrs. Bennett conceded tearfully. "Lydia did tell me about the documents -"

"Be quiet, Mrs. Bennett! You're incriminating yourself!"

"No, I can't lie anymore. But I didn't kill her, I swear. Please, just let me explain."

And Mrs. Bennett, ignoring the policeman's instruction to remain silent, started to talk.

"I don't have much money, just the pension, so when Mrs. Cohen was taken to hospital I thought she might die -"

And nobody else knew about the documents, thought Order.

"- and nobody except us knew about the documents," she said, looking up and seeking understanding from three stony-faced men.

"So I pretended there'd been a break-in and I stole," Mrs. Bennett faltered upon the word, "the papers. But then I couldn't understand them, they were in a foreign language. Polish, wasn't it? And I realised I couldn't do anything with them. Then Mrs. Cohen came back out of hospital. Losing her memory saved me because I could give them to you, Mr. Order, just as Lydia had intended and nobody would be any the wiser."

Mrs. Bennett leaned back into the lounge. "I was stupid to do such a thing," she admitted, shame showing upon her face, "but I didn't kill Lydia. Honest to God, she was dead when I found her."

"Then why take the tablets?" asked Order.

Mrs. Bennett looked away from him but remained silent, while Sergeant Shank's pen hovered over his notebook.

"We'll continue this at the station," said Williams, levering his bulk from the sagging lounge chair.

"D'you have family in Canberra, Mrs. Bennett?" Order said quickly.

And over an impatient growl from DI Williams, the old nurse agreed she did.

"Do I know them, Mrs. Bennett?" Order persisted.

"What's all this about, Mr. Order?" Williams questioned, but the old lady replied he did.

"Bob Bennett perhaps?"

"My nephew Robert, yes."

"Is that why you lied about me visiting Wednesday afternoon? Because of Bob an' his wife, Lorraine?"

Williams was listening intently and Shanks' pen was writing once more.

"Yes, it was," Mrs. Bennett said in a small voice. "I'm sorry Mr. Order, but I didn't think it would get you into so much trouble. They said you'd be able to explain it."

You lying old bitch, he thought, but it was no time to divert Mrs. Bennett with an angry attack upon her truthfulness.

"I understand," he said gently, "but perhaps we should start at the beginning. How did your nephew an' his wife get involved?"

"Robert's a good boy. He visits me from time to time; see how I'm getting on, y'know. They were terribly upset when Lorraine had to withdraw from the election. No offence Mr. Order, but blood's thicker than water and that untrue breast cancer scare you put around about Lorraine was, well, I thought better of you," she reproved. "But that's politics, I suppose."

"I told them I knew you and they wanted to know as much as possible about why I did. So I explained our involvement with Lydia. Robert thought there was something funny going on about those papers, Mr. Order, and asked me to keep him informed."

"After I found Lydia dead - and I swear I did," she added, with a nervous glance at Gabby Williams, "I was worried I might be blamed. As you know, this would be the second time I'd found her,

Mr. Order, and I thought it might be seen as too much of a coincidence. So I phoned Robert for advice."

"What time was this?" asked Williams. "When you found the deceased?"

"Early evening. About six or seven. It was dark."

So nobody saw you, decided Order.

"He agreed with me it wouldn't look good a second time and suggested I say I saw you there in the afternoon, Mr. Order. I'd seen you that morning, leaving the house with that other man?"

Order kept his eyes fixed upon Mrs. Bennett, wondering nevertheless who Williams was looking at.

"And so you told Sergeant Shanks when he visited you."

"Yes."

"You realise what this could have done to my career?"

"I was trying to help my nephew's wife, after the dirty trick you played on her, Mr. Order. And they said you'd be able to explain it. That you were somewhere else, with other people. You politicians lead such busy lives."

"Whose idea was taking the tablets?"

Mrs. Bennett hesitated.

"My own," she said finally. "I thought it might help."

"Enough," said Williams. "Sergeant, take Mrs. Bennett into Civic. We'll need a full statement, Mrs. Bennett."

"Yes, sir." Shanks was puzzled.

"Can you give me a lift to the station, Mr. Order? I'd like to talk with you."

"You were lucky, John," Gabby Williams said as Order drove along the quiet street.

"D'you reckon she decided to take the tablets? I don't."

"She'll stick to her story. It was a stupid thing to do and I'm not sure why she did so. Anyway, we'll never prove a crime has been committed."

"I know why, Gabby. If Mrs. Bennett had stuck to her story of seeing me that afternoon an' the tablets were missing, there'd be a strong suspicion I killed Mrs. Cohen. The motive being the papers in my briefcase. You mightn't be able to prove it, but that wouldn't matter. My political career would be over."

"On what we have, I'd say it would never get to court."

"No matter. No Party wants a candidate even suspected of something like murder. My people would take away my endorsement an' re-open preselection."

"And Bennett's wife would be a shoe-in?"

"You got it."

"And I think police work's tough."

"I reckon the Bennett's put her up to stealing the tablets too. That way she was in too deep to change her lie about Wednesday afternoon. They manipulated her more than she'll ever realise. But what now?"

"Not much. A statement, of course, for the coroner but no crime's been committed. Not perjury because it's not court sworn. False statement, wasting police time certainly, but she's hardly a habitual crim. Unless you want to press charges?"

"No way. No publicity is good publicity in this case. But d'you have to bring Mrs. Bennett in at all? The other woman found Lydia Cohen next day; do a few hours in not reporting the death really matter?"

"Probably an offence, but it would save a lot of paperwork if Mrs. Bennett didn't actually find her. Just couldn't raise her when she knocked on the door."

"You don't think she killed her?"

"No, I don't. Nurses, even old ones, don't usually kill people, notable serial exceptions aside, but the real defence is simply no motive."

"Greed?" Order succeeded in passing a white-knuckle driver hogging the centre lane of Commonwealth Avenue Bridge.

"Initially yes. But she found the documents were useless to her and then Mrs. Cohen recovered and she passed them onto you as the old lady had intended. She wouldn't have been vindictive about it and they *were* friends."

"So no motive?"

"No motive except to get even with you. But that's not a crime." Williams stared resolutely ahead as he spoke. "We'll give her a stern caution, of course."

The DI directed Order into the police parking area inside the security fence.

"I've still a couple of questions," he explained, so Order turned off the engine.

"Who was the other bloke Mrs. Bennett mentioned leaving with you on Wednesday morning from Mrs. Cohen's?"

"I thought you'd picked up on that," Order said resignedly, and told the policeman the story.

"Gabby, I don't think we need bring the Conrad's into this," he concluded. "I thought they were involved but obviously they're not."

"Nor do I, John," said the detective inspector, glaring off yet another uniformed officer about to move on Order's non-police vehicle parked in the reserved section. "Unnecessarily stir up powerful forces for both of us."

"Will you need these documents?" Order asked, with a nod at the briefcase at Williams' feet.

"No. We can keep that matter involving Mrs. Cohen separate from her death, but what are you going to do about Conrad? Give him the originals?"

"Don't see why I should. There are probably other claimants. Let him sweat."

Williams stirred and made to get out of the car. "How did you know about the Bennett relationship?"

"Lucky guess. Once I accepted Conrad was telling the truth an' his son had an alibi, there seemed nobody responsible for the break-in

- because that's what puzzled me - except maybe Mrs. Bennett. An' that required a motive."

"I'd probably have forgotten it, even when Lydia Cohen died, until I was put on the scene for the Wednesday afternoon visit an' the tablets were missing. Bennett is a fairly common name, of course, but equally Canberra's still fairly small. I'd wondered once or twice about a relationship but it wasn't important until I was being targeted. Then I realised old Mrs. Bennett could be Bob's mother or a relative an' they both lived in the older part of Canberra. In other words, they both could be long-time locals."

"Missed your vocation, didn't you," was all Williams said, but with a rare smile.

A sandwich lunch at his desk, winnowing the in-tray papers, his dedication to the task keeping the ever sensitive Liz away from him, his activity finally broken by a mid-afternoon telephone call from Gabby Williams.

"How's Mrs. Bennett?"

"Made a satisfactory statement."

Maybe Williams only really was laconic in police stations, thought Order.

"Did she have Mrs. Cohen's copy of the translated papers?"

"Yep."

"So what now?"

"So nothing. As far as we can determine, Mrs. Cohen died alone of a heart attack sometime Wednesday afternoon."

"So that's it?"

"Yes and no. About Mrs. Cohen, yes. Everything and everyone around her recently is interesting, including those old papers, but has no direct bearing from a police point of view upon her death."

"And the no?" In spite of his anger with the Bennett family, the arrogant Conrad and his delinquent son, Order was relieved.

"The no is we've at last heard from Israel. Our man in Tel Aviv finally tracked down someone who knew Daniel Levy. A girlfriend, we understand, who'd been on holiday. Anyway, she confirmed Levy's parents are dead and he has no known relatives. According to this girlfriend, Levy used his savings to come to Australia. He wanted her to come with him but she preferred Europe."

"Remarkably well informed."

"We've been pushing hard, John," said Williams with an edge to his voice and then his tone lightened: "Levy's an accidental death, by the way, so it's all finished. Take care."

Sitting cradling the dead telephone receiver yet again, Order thought of Daniel Levy, Lydia Cohen, old now unrealised fortune-making documents, a Warsaw building with a lift and oak leaves thick upon Canberra's suburban nature strips.

"No, you're wrong, Gabby," he said quietly. "It will never be finished."

www.ingramcontent.com/pod-product-compliance
Lightning Source LLC
Chambersburg PA
CBHW020333260626
47156CB00004B/1509